A
CLOWN
IN THE
MOONLIGHT

A CLOWN IN THE MOONLIGHT

by JAMES HOWARD KUNSTLER

St. Martin's Press
New York

Copyright © 1981 by James Howard Kunstler
For information, write: St. Martin's Press,
175 Fifth Avenue, New York, N.Y. 10010
Manufactured in the United States of America

Library of Congress Cataloging in Publication Data

Kunstler, James Howard.
    A clown in the moonlight.

    I. Title.
PS3561.U55C5   813'.54   80-29382
ISBN O-312-14495-4

Design by Manuela Paul
10 9 8 7 6 5 4 3 2 1
First Edition

This book is for John Koch

*There's nothing funny about
a clown in the moonlight.*

—Lon Chaney

one

HUMAN NATURE: The nature of man is familiar, impressively unique and almost indescribable.

—The Encyclopedia Britannica

You want hard facts? Sometimes you have to get to the truth through the back door. Look up BABOON instead. It says here that the baboon (genus *Papio*) is a large, robust monkey who is a destructive and dangerous adversary, and is capable of communicating via shrieks, barks, and flauntings of the hindquarters. He is considered *highly intelligent* and *educable*.

Now I think we're getting somewhere—certainly closer to the beginning of our story, in Reddington, Vermont, where for a few brief, hallucinatory seasons I taught English at America's most exclusive college for women.

The idea that man is just a monkey with clothes on is a relatively new one, more recent, in fact, than the ideas of democracy, of algebra, crop rotation, double-entry bookkeeping, painless dentistry, the salad fork, the steamboat, the howitzer, or the notion that we pass this

1

way but once. Like many truthful ideas, it is deceptively simple ("A penny saved is a penny earned." "Nice guys finish last." "Cigarette Smoking Is Dangerous to Your Health.") Also, like many truthful ideas, it is hard for some people to swallow. (I spent the better part of last Saturday morning arguing about evolution with two doorbell-ringing Jehovah's Witnesses (they were against it) who stupidly selected me as a target for their propaganda. I love to get sassy with religious nuts.)

Anyway, it says here that the whole baboon society is based on satisfying the whims of dominant males, these whims being largely sexual in content. The baboon society, therefore, is a simpler model of our own, as the baboon's brain is a simpler version of man's, lacking only man's characteristic wishes, dreams, goals, schemes, plans, and Big Ideas. Spared these daunting infelicities, the baboon's brain exists only to send a continuous stream of urgent directives to his pelvis, thus assuring infinite generations of little baboons. Being an ape means never having to say you're sorry.

I suppose that there are a great many things I am sorry about, but my crimes at Reddington are not among them. My transformation from genus *Homo* to genus *Papio*, begun there, is now resoundingly complete. As metamorphoses go, mine was quite a number.

There I was: such a clever young fellow on the footpath to success, married, a gut job in a bucolic Vermont wonderland, my future penny-bright and dollar-safe. Beware the surfaces of things. Life is not all it's cracked up to be in the graduate school career clubs. Beneath the surface of *my* life was something like Conan Doyle's vision of the center of the earth, a swampy bestiary of primitive emotions packed with giant hairy spiders of depravity, lurching lizards of lust, swooping pterodactyls of resentment, and spooky little red-eyed rodents of jealousy and revenge. Also, one baboon. My first apprehension of this inner nether world wasn't nearly that vivid, of course. I sensed it as a kind of distant soundtrack of jungle yammering, a faraway mumbo jumbo of weird animal squawks, barely noticeable like music in the supermarket.

But with the passage of time, and various demoralizing events, the volume got louder. I couldn't turn it off. At one point I figured if I could only just name it, it might go away. "Unresolved Oedipal Conflict" had a nice ring. "Occupational Stress" lacked weight and importance. "Death Anxiety" showed some promise and fizzled. There were lots more—big chewy theoretical figments from the pop-psychology grab-bag. The exorcism failed.

For a while I thought it might be some rare but innocuous disease, an invasion of unusually noisy bacteria, and tried to ignore it as the veterans of the diplomatic corps ignore the pesky but harmless tropical amoebas that creep into their veins and swim there for a lifetime. Luckily we were in the middle of an era when everybody and his uncle was striving to uncover his roots. And just as surely as the Afro-American embraced his blackness, or as persons of the female ilk rejoiced in their sisterhood, as Poles, Italians, Samoans, Latvians, Croatians, Puerto Ricans reveled in their endemic charms, achievements and endowments, so did I, Richie Schuster, thirty-year-old middle-class gringo fuckhead, discover my debt to the baboon—my baboon heritage! What a relief. But this awareness didn't spring full-blown overnight. It arrived in stages.

I remember one exemplary spell of confusion. It was after one of the innumerable and ridiculous fights Sally and I were having at the time. I was raking leaves in the front yard of our college-owned campus residence, when two little buds from my Thoreau seminar wheeled down the lane on their Japanese racing bikes, spines arched and peach-cleft bottoms lifted against the azure sky to reveal (on one of them anyway) golden tufts of pubic hair at the juncture of thighs and gym shorts.

This mild encounter left me positively unhinged, breathless with what I failed to recognize was simple desire. My hands shook so badly that the tines of my leaf rake jangled below like a cheap wind harp. Jungle noises raced through my skull. I was losing it, fast.

It was poor Chesmire, the psychiatrist, who finally pointed me in the right direction—the gifted, but reckless, Chesmire, with his slight Scots burr, his functional furniture, and his Earth Shoes, who led me sternly by the hand through those dismal glades of hysteria where the sun never shines to the more spacious groves of my mind's heart. Brilliant, wicked, unfortunate Chesmire. He had a fix on the ineluctable mechanics of human behavior which made someone like Jesus Christ, with all his drippy little bonbons of goodness, seem about as bright as the Cracker Jack boy. Not that I worshiped him. In fact, he wasn't even very likeable. But when I came to Chesmire with my magazine-derived theories of "mental illness," he cut right to the heart of the matter.

"Unresolved oedipal conflict?" he asked.

"Uh, that's right."

"What is it?"

"You know, the mother-father . . . *thing.*"

"Oh," he said. "What mother-father thing?"

"You know, the *thing,* with your mother and father."

"The thing with my mother and father?"

"No, *my* mother and father."

"Are you trying to tell me that your life isn't working?"

"My life? No. It's my head."

"I see."

"My psyche."

"Oh. But it's not connected with your life?"

"Of course it's connected. You have to live in your

head. Your nerves all lead there, right? It's my nerves."

"Oh, your nerves."

"Yeah, the nerves in my head."

"What's wrong with the nerves in your head?"

"Death anxiety."

"Death anxiety? Is that like the oedipal thing?"

"No, it's different."

"What is it?"

"It's . . . are you kidding me?"

"I'm not kidding you."

"You don't know what that is?"

"I'm very interested to hear what you think it is."

"The *thing*. Where you worry about death. Only it's so frightening that you don't even know it's death that you're actually worrying about. So, you worry about stupid little things instead."

"In your life?"

"Of course in your life. How can you worry about death unless you're alive?"

"But you're worried about stupid little things, not death."

"It's really death, though, underneath."

"How can you be sure?"

"Because I never think about death. It must be what I'm really worried about."

At this point, the other members of the group started chuckling and tittering. I forgot to tell you: I wasn't alone with him in some office. It was group therapy, and this whole humiliating exchange was going on in front of five other people. As chance would have it, they were all women.

"You're dumping on me," I said.

"I'm dumping on you?" Chesmire said. "Look what you just dumped on me: death anxiety! Unresolved oedipal . . . what was that?"

"Conflict. *Con*-flict!"

"Yccch, all over me."

"It wasn't my intention to pay fifty dollars to get dumped on. And laughed at."

"Great!" Chesmire said. "Only an asshole would pay to get dumped on. It's a great stride forward for you to recognize that."

"Maybe I'd better leave."

"It's a real option."

"You're telling me to leave."

"I'm telling you no such thing. It was your idea."

"But you don't care if I do."

"Realistically speaking, no."

"Great. Then I'll leave."

But I didn't. I got out of my seat . . . but just stood there. Then, I said to the others, "That's what you pay him for, huh? To sit here and be called assholes?"

"Sometimes," one of the women said. She was a semiattractive redhead in a pantsuit. There was a yellowish black contusion under her left eye, a fading shiner, actually.

"So, you call them assholes and that's supposed to help them, huh?" I turned to Chesmire.

"Are you a lawyer?" another woman asked.

"What? No, I'm not a lawyer."

"I thought you might be a lawyer."

"And why would you think I was a lawyer?"

"You act like you're trying to defend us against him."

"Well, I'm not a lawyer, in case you're interested."

"Then I'll thank you to not take responsibility for me," the woman said.

"I'm not trying to take— oh, this is ridiculous."

"Rough on your nerves?" a third woman inquired.

"He's supposed to help people!" I raved, pointing at Chesmire.

"Who says?" Chesmire retorted.

"You're a doctor, aren't you? You took the Hippocratic oath, didn't you?"

"Yes. So . . . ?"

"It says you're supposed to help people."

"It lies. I can tell them only what they already know. Have a seat and stick around for a while."

Don't ask me why I stayed. I was so upset by then that I guess I was afraid to leave. For the rest of the time Chesmire and the group pretty much ignored me and my problems and I sat there like a bump on a log listening to everybody else. For some reason, it was curiously uplifting.

This, then, was the beginning of my association with Chesmire the psychiatrist. And it continued, to my increasing profit, until he died by his own devices ten months later.

two

It was a dream come true.

Sally and I arrived in Reddington late on a late summer's day in '73—that "purple hour" of the day, in the words of the late Bernard De Voto, when the sun is low upon the hills, and the shadows are long, and the birds are down from the high meadow and singing, and the surface of the earth is at its loveliest.

Our decrepit Volvo was packed to the scuppers like one of those jitney buses which ply the mountain roads of Mexico. Entanglements of clothesline secured our possessions to a rusted luggage rack. The ladder-back of a favorite rocking chair stuck out of a rear window. We were parked in the driveway of the handsome and ancient white clapboard farmhouse we were about to move into. A few late hollyhocks bloomed in the high grass near a weed patch that had obviously been another couple's garden. The remnant of a swing (one rope attached to a warped and weathered board) hung in the breezeless air from the stout limb of a maple tree, its leaves just showing the slightest tips of scarlet. *(Soon, a child of our own?*) The whole scene looked like the cover of a *Vermont Life* magazine. We stood there together on the lawn, arm in arm, for a very long time, speechless, until tears welled in our eyes, as if this tidy little pastoral stage set could really be ours! It really was, for all practical purposes. We were still standing there when the sun went down.

You see, you have to understand where we were coming from. For many years we lived in the more unpleasant districts of various major cities while I faked and fussed my way through a series of academic degrees in American Literature (AmLit). First there was Washington, D.C., by far the easiest station along that difficult pilgrimage. But I'll bypass that part of our history for now.

Next there was New York, our Hieronymus Bosch interlude. We lived in a fourth-story walk-up on 124th Street and Claremont Avenue in Harlem, where Columbia University shakes hands with the Black Experience. Until near the end, I was much too busy working on my thesis to fully comprehend just how bad it really was. For some reason the vestibule of our building was the elephants' graveyard of the neighborhood, where derelicts crawled off to die. I stumbled over half a dozen of them in a year, and it became my official duty to notify the cops and their medical pals. I signed the documents while they scooped the remains of these poor mothers' sons into plastic bags for convenient disposal. This was only part of the program for keeping you on your toes in the Big Apple. There were other earthly delights involving run-ins with surly strangers in the hallways, heart-piercing screams issuing from the air shaft at three in the morning, and courtesy calls by rip-off artists, junkies, perverts and other local riffraff. One in particular springs to mind as I recollect those grim days.

It was nine-thirty on a weekday morning. Sally was

already off to her job with the NYC parole board. I happened to be home, working at my desk in the spare bedroom we used as an office, when the doorbell rang. Our door had about 116 locks on it, including this steel bar that you jammed into the floor. But it had no peephole.

"Yeah? Who is it?" I yelled through the door.

"It's the meter reader," a male voice replied.

"Meter reader . . .?"

"Yeah."

"Whaddaya want?"

"Read the meter."

"Look, we don't have any meter."

"Yes you do. I'll show you."

"Forget it."

"The super sent me."

"How do I know you're the meter reader?"

"Would I lie to you?"

I shrank away from the door as from some Satanic altar. Maybe I exaggerate, but at the time, the metaphysical weight of that final question was too heavy for me to handle. Or it could be more accurate to state that it represented the culmination of all the dangerous absurdities that crowded our fragile existence there. Anyway, I called the cops on the sucker, but he was gone by the time they got there. Luckily he did not ring my bell again.

Then, the week before Christmas, our apartment was entered and burgled for the third and final time. We had been away at Sally's parents' place in Maryland for the weekend. Most of our stuff was packed in crates because we were about to move to Cambridge. A few of them were ripped open to reveal . . . *books!*—to the evident displeasure of our thief, who peed and made potty in the center of our bed to show what he thought of us as victims. Otherwise, all he got was a cheap clock radio, his predecessors having already bagged a TV, our stereo, a typewriter, and every other negotiable item on hand.

It still seems like a miracle that we got out of there alive. I was mugged twice during that period—once in front of our building and another time just a few steps from the entrance of the West End bar. The first time, I resisted and got stomped into the sidewalk. The second time, I decided to play it smart and hand the wallet right over. The teenage banditos called me a *chocha* and a *maricón* and stomped me anyway, just for the sheer fun of it.

Sally got off pretty easy, considering. Her purse was snatched once on the subway, so she wisely quit carrying one. On a winter evening our second year there, she was pestered by a wino who liked to camp out in the vestibule of our building. A swift kick from one of Sally's logging boots sent him reeling through the door into the slushy streets, clutching his sclerotic old nuts, to darken our hallway nevermore. She was mighty proud of her grit under pressure that night, and who can blame her?

Anyway, it was farewell to the heart of darkness and hello to the heart of deepness: Cambridge, Mass., city of golden domes, electric trolleys, small cafés, bookstores, sensible furniture, omelette pans, Big Ideas, and Hugo movies. It was here, at a highly regarded diploma-mill, that I prepared my PhD dissertation (or, as Sally, the Dean Swift of Central Square, liked to put it, my defecation) on transportation imagery in late-nineteenth- and early-twentieth-century AmLit—a real gem! Sally got a job in the Food Stamp division of the welfare office, helping the US Department of Agriculture subsidize the bomb plots of slumming, rich-kid revolutionaries (thanks to federal confiscations from the paychecks of genuine poor working slobs). But to be fair about it, Sally supported us, without complaining, in spite of the fact that her father was a wealthy, retired Maryland congressman, whose occasional offers of "help" we both idiotically refused on grounds of principle which seem insane in hindsight.

I put in my fair share of time with the old AmLit on excellent methedrine furnished by my jocose pal, Paul Krezney, a law student, squash partner and drinking buddy. Sally and I rented a squalid apartment on Hancock Street, off Central Square, in an out-of-plumb wooden tenement redecorated in motifs of sea water-colored Congoleum and pressboard "knotty pine" paneling. The bedroom was exactly large enough for our rehabilitated bed and nothing else. So we kept our dressers in the kitchen, the biggest room we had, and our clothing always reeked of sesame oil from Sally's experiments in Chinese cooking. But the place cost us only $75 a month, and for all our griping we never made an effort to find something better. Also, for some bizarre reason (possibly all the speed I was using) I actually believed we were happy together there.

Ours was a life of humble pleasures. Our recreations were mainly free ones—frisbeeing on the commons with Krezney and his plump wench, bicycling along the Charles, browsing in the bookstalls. There were Chinese dinners cooked by Sally and shared, too frequently, with Sally's office chum, Lisette, and Lisette's dyke girlfriend "Mike"—sort of a hulking golem who ruined the only party we ever gave by throwing a jealous fit and upending a buffet table.

About once a week, we went to the movies. Now I happen to like rather violent movies, myself, with lots of blood and gore and broken heads and gunshot wounds—for reasons I have only lately begun to understand. Sally, on the other hand, was addicted to these depressing thirty-year-old *film-noir* French flicks featuring a character named Hugo always wandering around the foggy docks of Marseilles looking for another character named Hugo who stole his girl Marie. Notwithstanding the different-strokes-for-different-folks theory of art appreciation, I couldn't stand these fucking movies, and Sally always dragged me along, and I was too chicken to say "no." Secretly, I think Sally made me go as a punishment for banning Lisette and Mike from our apartment. I would have slept through them, except for all that meth dancing around in my bloodstream. They were always in black and white too, these Hugo movies, and the theater was always packed as if the management gave out merit badges for arduous brain-work.

And you should have heard the conversations in the lobby after the show. The catch-words were "in terms of." You see, in the university world nothing has any ontological substance of its own; it always has to be stated "in terms of" something else. "Society's debt to the criminal *in terms of* . . . ." "Hugo's relationship with Marie *in terms of* . . . ." I'd rather go see *Dirty Harry* or something where at least when somebody gets shot in the face you know it's *in terms of* Harry being pissed off.

Not that I made a big issue of it. I just kept my mouth shut and went along for the ride. Once, I snuck across the river to Tremont Street to catch *The Godfather*, which Sally considered "too violent" to dignify with her attendance. On the way back, on the MTA, you could see fog creeping over the Charles, and for a few minutes I was afraid I was turning into a Hugo myself, that my life itself was turning into a black-and-white Hugo movie. After that, I decided to cut down somewhat on the speed.

Anyway, we managed, mainly happily I thought, through all the vicissitudes of Cambridge life and my degree-getting, and a general shortage of funds, and too much speed, and our crummy apartment, and all the fried rice we ate, and the Hugo movies, and the hot summers and the cold winters, and by March of our second year I was up to my eyeballs in job applications.

The job picture looked pretty grim, to tell you the

truth. We were in the middle of a recession. The post-World War II baby-boom was winding down, and undergraduate enrollments were off all over the place. To make it worse, products of that baby-boom like myself were being cranked out of the graduate schools in a bumper crop, and the teaching market was glutted with young PhD's. Still, I was committed to an academic career and didn't want to think about the alternatives. So, in the late winter of that year I shotgunned about a hundred colleges and universities, and even a few prep schools, with letters of inquiry about a teaching job. (It was a well-known fact, meanwhile, that several Harvard PhD's were pumping gas at various Cambridge filling stations, and I personally got to know one guy with a PhD in education who washed dishes at the Orson Welles restaurant.)

Out of these one hundred-odd inquiries I got nineteen responses asking to hear more from me. Out of these nineteen, five were interested in talking to me personally. That April and May, I spent our small savings on plane tickets to such places as Tulane, the University of Indiana, the University of Minnesota, Northwestern University, and Case Western Reserve in Cleveland. Notice that Reddington was not among them.

At each of these schools I got the same story: they didn't have any immediate openings, but they were interviewing in case *funding* turned up. (Back in those days of the Nixon Administration there was still a lot of loose federal cash in the bureaucratic thickets. It merely had to be rooted out by trained flunkies, the way French farmers root out truffles with trained pigs.) Anyway, after these five, futile airplane rides, *our* funding was dried up, and Sally and I were broke.

At the end of May, I had my comps and orals and spent three solid weeks locked in a cubicle in the basement of the Widener Library, drilling. With all job prospects shot to hell, I nurtured this fantasy: right after my orals I would calmly denounce the educational system for foiling my hopes and dreams, and dooming me to a life of pumping gas; I would pull out a .357 magnum revolver, wave it around the room until everybody got good and paranoid, and then blow my brains out, soiling the tweeds of each faculty member with pink flecks of brain tissue, which, an instant before, had contained mini-bits of data on the subject of AmLit (as well as a billion random memories—a pony ride, Don Larson's "perfect" game, my first hand-job).

Then, the day before my actual orals, paranoia cresting, I returned to the apartment to scarf down a bowl of Cheerios and found a letter in the mailbox from Reddington College—one of the original one hundred-odd. The letter apologized for taking so long. But not only did it ask me to come for an interview, it came right out and said that there was an opening in the English department, and added that they were impressed with my credentials. I was stunned. I staggered upstairs and slurped down my lunch with the letter spread out on the table, rereading its few meagre sentences over and over and over. The rest of what happened that week is shrouded in my memory with a thick Hugo-like fog. My orals were like watching a movie of someone else taking his orals. A Vincent Price movie.

I drove to Reddington on the following Thursday and interviewed with various deans and President Bleeker and with Dr. Royce, chairman of the department. They even asked me to stick around an extra day to meet the other members of the English faculty, and had a little reception for me at the departmental office. Near the end, Dr. Royce steered me into an alcove and asked if I would accept a starting salary of $19,500. He added parenthetically that the nineteen five happened to come with a rent-free residence in a college-owned farmhouse, which might make the offer sweeter than it seemed.

I did a stupid thing. I told Dr. Royce I'd have to "think it over" and that I'd call him in a few days from Cambridge when I reached a decision. Don't ask me what inspired this game of hard-to-get, as if I had a dozen other offers to sift through. It was just sort of a reflex response, possibly the result of watching too many TV shows. And though I instantly regretted it, I couldn't very well take it back, could I, without seeming to be a complete asshole. "Let me think it over and call you back in a few days." What a schmuck.

Driving back along Route 2 that night, I just about fractured my skull from banging my head against the steering wheel of the Volvo. I was too ashamed to tell Sally what happened. Instead, I just acted real spooky and told her I had to go hiking in the mountains for a few days alone and think things over. I didn't go hiking. I left my backpack in the goddam closet. But I didn't call Royce back immediately, either, and accept the job, because I figured I had to play out the stupid bluff to the end.

What I did was hole up in Krezney's apartment for two days watching television, listening to him dog his fat girlfriend while I flirted with thoughts of suicide. Then, on Monday morning at nine o'clock, I sat in one of Krezney's cruddy, roach-infested easy chairs with the phone in my lap and waited until it felt right to call. I started dialing at 9:45, but changed my mind and slammed the receiver down. I didn't want to appear anxious (ha ha!). Finally at 10:15 I put the call through. Dr. Royce's secretary said he was in class and asked to take a message.

"No message!" I stammered. "When do you expect him back?"

She said not until after lunch, about 1:30. I hung up, lurched into the kitchen and mindlessly devoured an entire half-gallon of Krezney's pistachio ice-cream. I turned on the TV and changed the channel about fifty times. I did push-ups for a while. I composed suicide notes and ripped them up. I huddled in Krezney's foul waterless bathtub with my head between my knees and blubbered like a baby. Somehow, I got through the morning. At a quarter to two, I placed another call and the secretary put me through to Dr. Royce.

"Hi," I said, casual as hell, as if I just got off the golf course. "This is Richard Schuster."

"Oh my, yes, Schuster. We'd just about given up hope on you."

Death knells: *gong gong gong.* I imagined some other young doctoral candidate sitting right there in Royce's office that very moment, some Teutonic marvel of breeding from Princeton with perfect teeth, a blinding smile of confidence, and a list of publications as long as your arm. In a parallel vein, I pictured all the prescription bottles in Krezney's medicine chest and wondered which was the fastest, the least painful, the most lethal.

"I said, we'd just about given up hope on you, my boy."

"Hunh—?"

"Hearing from you, I mean."

"Oh? Uh, yes. Sorry. Must be a bad connection at my end. Can you hear me, Dr. Royce? Can—"

"Yes, perfectly."

"You can? Uh, Dr. Royce, I've been thinking about your offer, and I've decided that it would be an honor to join the faculty at Reddington."

"Frankly, Richard, we were a little disappointed—"

New waves of panic and despair. Murderous rolling breakers like the Banzai pipeline.

"What did you say, Richard?"

I think I was whimpering, like a gerbil.

"N-n-nothing, Dr. Royce."

"We were kind of surprised that you didn't snap up our offer right on the spot. But I guess a young fellow in your position might want to take extra special care in a decision of this sort."

"It'll be an honor for me to join the faculty at Reddington," I repeated myself stupidly like a goddam tape recorder.

"Fine. Fine. Glad to hear it, Schuster. And the feeling's mutual. I know I speak for all my colleagues here. I'll have my secretary notify Dean Lansing's secretary to send you the contract. It's our standard one-year renewable. If you have any questions, don't hesitate to call me. Call collect if you like. I can imagine what a struggle it's been, young man."

"Gee. Thanks, sir."

"And say, why don't you and your wife come up for a weekend—uh, Saturday before the Fourth of July. I'm sorry, what did you say your wife's name was . . .?"

"Uh, Sally."

"Yes. Well, why don't you and Sally come up then. We're—heh heh—a pretty informal institution, you know. We prefer an informal orientation. Come up for the weekend, and we'll square away your living arrangements, take you around to meet the rest of the guys and gals, bend an elbow—heh heh—you know, get to know each other. What do you say?"

"It'll be an honor to join the faculty at Reddington." What a jerk!

"Yes. Well, okay then. Saturday before the Fourth. In fact, Friday night might be even better. I'll tell Peggy to lay in provisions. If I know you ambitious young fellows like I think I do, I'll bet you haven't had a nice, relaxing weekend in the country for a long time."

"It's had its hours of darkness, sir. That's very kind of you."

"Think nothing of it. I'm sure we'll have a grand time. Uh, what did you say your wife's name was again?"

"Sally."

"Sorry, I'm a perfect mongo for names."

"A what, sir?"

"A mongo. A mongoloid idiot. Well, nice talking with you, Richard, and glad to have you aboard. See you the Friday before the Fourth."

"Right. And thank you, sir."

"Bye." Click.

"Bye. . . ."

I lowered the receiver back into its cradle as if it were made out of blown glass and sat in the dimness of Krezney's hootchy rat hole for a long time, perfectly still. Slowly it began to dawn on me: my troubles were over, *our* troubles were over, I had a job! We had it made in the shade.

I limped out of Krezney's building into the blinding sunlight for the first time in about forty-eight hours. Brattle Street was suddenly transformed from a war zone of battling omelette pans to the lane of some renaissance fair. A Bluegrass band was playing on the corner of Mt. Auburn. Even the panhandlers in Harvard Square seemed different, more like winsome clowns than scungy semipsychotic pests. "Spare change?" "You bet!" I was weightless with happiness and floated down Massachusetts Avenue to Hancock Street like a balloon in the Macy's Thanksgiving Day Parade.

Through those hardbitten years of city life in Washington, New York and Cambridge, our big dream was always to escape to the country. Not just the country, you understand, but The Country: that spanking-clean, evergreen figment of the magazine industry and the latter-day Gringo imagination where it is always Sunday in May, and the birdies always sing, and where, if the skies just happen to be cloudy all day, you make gingerbread, or sit out on the porch and whittle. To us, as well as a lot of other fuckheads, The Country, strictly speaking, always

meant Vermont, where that corpus of lost causes known
as The Arts coexists with the humble moo-cow life in ideal
harmony. Any fool could see that the life available in
other states, however rural or toilsome, was not, properly
speaking, The Country, because in those awful places the
farmers painted their antique houses turquoise and
pink—or else torched them for the insurance and hauled a
mobile home onto the property. They were therefore and
obviously not Real Farmers, and any fool could tell that
theirs was not really The Country. In The Country, one
paints one's house white and one's barn red. Violators
will be prosecuted. Life in The Country revolves around
the Little Village. Its townspeople are curiously sophisti-
cated and well-dressed, if still folksy in their locutions.
There are half a dozen book shops on Main Street. Also, a
liquor store, a hardware store that sells gourmet kitchen
equipment as well as manure forks, and a "general store"
where you can get a bag of bagels, a half-pound of first-
class Nova, and the Sunday *New York Times*. Now, that's
The Country, pardner.

On Sundays in Cambridge, while Sally slept off the
effects of her job, it was my duty to slip off to the
newsstand on Harvard Square and pick up the *Times* and
the *Globe*. I also usually bought the latest issues of *Yankee*,
Vermont Life, *Organic Gardening*, *Mother Earth News*, and
other guild publications of The Country. For Sally, I told
myself.

But, the truth is, I too was nurtured by those
photographs of Country roads overhung with gold and
scarlet leaves, those informative articles on how to install
your woodstove, those display ads for "old-timey" ker-
osene lamps, wheels of "home-made" cheddar, Shaker
furniture kits, bird feeders, quilts, log splitters, andirons,
roto-tillers, mulchers, chain-saws, cheese balls, hams,
jams, and other indispensable stage-props of our future
life in The Country.

On Sunday afternoons Sally baked cookies and pies from recipes in *The Old Farmer's Almanac*. We prepped ourselves for a return to some fuckhead version of the nineteenth century where the air was always clean and there was always plenty of invigorating work to be done (bringing in the pumpkin harvest!) but which also happily included a few twentieth-century diversions and amenities like movies and root canals.

Way back in New York, we bought twin backpacks, sleeping bags and hiking boots with one of Sally's windfall tax refunds. I think we used them a couple of times. The best part was bringing them home from the store when they were new and playing with the buckles and straps. The Woods, we later learned, made you smelly, cold, wet and uncomfortable. But the Woods were not the same thing as The Country where, at least, you could take a bath and sleep in a warm dry place.

On Sunday nights, Sally and I curled up in bed with steaming mugs of hot cocoa "made from scratch!" and all our Country catalogs scattered about the quilt. Sally, my tender Country maiden. Wearing only woolen hiking socks, lace panties, and one of my giant Pendleton shirts, Sally systematically circled items in the L.L. Bean wish book with a yellow highlighter pen while I studied an agricultural bulletin. But it was impossible not to avert my eyes from, say, that informative article on how to dig your own root cellar to the warm cave that Sally made with her large breasts inside the carelessly buttoned shirt. I put her cocoa mug down on the floor beside my own, reached over and slipped off her panties, and rode her like an inflatable raft down the burbling waters of a Country stream. Merrily, merrily, in bitter Cambridge, we made sweet Country love.

A few hours after that fateful phone call to Dr. Royce, I was back in the apartment waiting for Sally to come home from work so I could break the news. Sitting quietly in one of our Goodwill Industries loungers, I had already put a considerable dent in a bottle of cheap California champagne, and there was another bottle of the real stuff, Piper Heidsieck, waiting in the fridge. Trying to maintain myself at a nice even plateau of intoxication, I was busy stuffing some weed in the bowl of a pipe when I heard her footsteps coming up the stairs. The key clicked in the door. When she saw me, all the features of her face crowded together to form a mask of indignation.

"Getting stoned?" she said, eyeing the pipe.

"You bet!" I told her cheerfully. But she just stalked into the kitchen where I heard her chuck her keys down on the kitchen table. Next thing I knew, I could hear the shower running. In the heat of events, I had failed to consider the effects of my weird disappearance. All my rehearsals about breaking the news suddenly went out the window. Ten minutes later you could tell she was still fuming the way she slammed the dresser drawers shut. I couldn't figure out how to tell her, and the weed and wine weren't helping at this point.

"It's a good thing you're freshening up because we're going out for dinner," I said.

She came out of the kitchen in her panties and a cotton top and just stood there glaring at me for a moment.

"What do you mean 'we,' white man? I'm going to Legal Seafood with Lisette and you are *not* invited."

"Is Mike going?"

"I don't know. Probably. Why?"

"We could double-date."

"Ha ha."

I should have known it was no time to get cute around that sore subject. Sally stormed back into the kitchen to finish dressing.

"Hey, I got that job, Sally."

There was silence from the kitchen. She stopped moving, at least.

"Did you hear me? I said I got the job."

This time I heard her sort of pad over to the doorway. She peeked in cautiously.

"I beg your pardon," she said.

"I got the job. At Reddington College."

"In Vermont?"

"No, in American Samoa. Yeah, in Vermont!"

"Did you eat those peyote buttons in the freezer?"

"You think I'm hallucinating?"

"It doesn't hurt to ask."

"I spoke to the chairman this afternoon. He's sending the contracts in the mail. I start in September. They even give us a farmhouse to live in. A farmhouse, for Chrissake, Sally, a farmhouse!"

Sally looked pale. She staggered over to our Salvation Army sofa and sat down.

"You got the job?" she said meekly.

"That's what I'm trying to tell ya, ya cluck!"

Slowly, her face seemed to fill with light, as if she was outside and the sun just came out from behind a cloud to shine on it.

"You got the job!" she cried. The next moment we were both hopping up and down, like one of us just hit a home run in the last game of the world series, and a moment after that I was spraying a forty-two-dollar bottle of champagne all over us.

That night we left Lisette and Mike to their own mysterious devices. I called up Anthony's Pier 4 in Boston and made reservations for eight-thirty. We wrote out a check for $100 and went down to the corner liquor store to cash it. The old guy who ran the place didn't want to do it, but I gave him my whole goddam wallet to hold for security and he forked over the dough.

It was much later, after lobster and popovers and a lot more wine, that Sally broke some interesting news of her own.

"I had an abortion today, Rich."

"Uh, what . . .?"

"I had an abortion today."

"An abortion?"

"Yes."

"Why?"

She looked at me blankly for a moment.

"I was pregnant, Rich."

"You were?"

She nodded her head.

"When did you get pregnant?"

She sighed and hesitated. "A couple of months ago, I guess." She looked back at me and made a kind of helpless little face.

"I didn't know you were pregnant."

"I didn't want you to get upset."

"I wouldn't have got upset."

"I thought you might be."

"I wouldn't have."

"I was afraid you might."

For a long time we didn't say anything.

"Are you angry at me?" she asked.

"Angry? No, I'm not angry. Are you all right?"

"I'm okay. It's a pretty quick procedure. You go in pregnant and you come out not pregnant. I didn't mind it that much. The doctor told me to take it easy for a few days, but I feel okay. Please don't be angry, Rich. It just wasn't the time for it, that's all."

I didn't know what to say. I wasn't even quite sure what I felt exactly—sad, certainly, but other emotions lurked silently behind the sadness. I was afraid to risk discovering what they were. Instead, I just reached across the table, took Sally's hands, and just sort of rubbed and patted them.

"There'll be time," I told her quietly. "There'll be time in the country."

three

From the first day, I detected in the air around Reddington the distinct fragrance of sea water. We were a good six-hour drive from the ocean, but the appealing stink was clear and unmistakable. In a while I shall tell you what it was.

According to Gluck's College Directory (1977 edition) Reddington College is the most expensive college in the United States. Tuition and fees for a regular thirty credit-hour year works out to roughly $5,400. Room and board, which is mandatory for all but a handful of married and special students, runs another $3,700. Simple arithmetic shows that this works out to $9,100 (not including spending money or incidentals) or a whopping $36,400 for a bachelor's degree—which is roughly what my folks paid for a whole goddam house on Long Island when I was in grade school.

At 9,100 simoleons a year Reddington is a pretty exclusive school too. The student body is, shall we say, not all that heterogeneous. In fact, it wasn't until 1971 that it accepted any male students, and since then only a token handful. There is a widespread rumor that they are all queers. This is unfair and untrue. There are a few squirrels among them, even a few nurds, but most of Reddington's fifty-odd male students are as straight as Doberman pinschers and as happy as pigs in clover.

On the other hand, Reddington has a long-standing reputation as a hotbed of lesbianism. If so, then it is very much a consequence of the school's peculiar history and not just the fads of the day. Reddington College, for all its Hepplewhite furniture and ersatz venerable Yankee ambience, was founded as recently as 1923. Nor was it cut from the same scratchy old conservative cloth as the other Yankee girls' colleges it seems to resemble. Let's take a short detour down memory lane and see how it came to be.

Reddington College was born when a flaky old free-thinking ex-Utopian spinster named Eleanor Hayes Tichnor kicked the bucket in the 1920s and left her property and considerable fortune toward the establishment of a college for women. However, this Tichnor did not just leave her will to the fates of greedy relatives and government tax agents. She was a sharp old bird and wise enough to know that most wills, following probate, tend to transform liquifiable assets into round-the-world cruises taken by pinhead nieces, new Cadillacs in the driveways of no-account nephews, and public works revenues in state and federal treasuries. No, this Tichnor saw to everything before she went, personally supervising the first stages of the conversion of her property into an institution of higher learning.

She hired its first president, Eugene Huntington Shanks (a visionary dean cashiered by the University of Pennsylvania's Wharton School for his promotion of world government, and more specifically, his sponsor-

ship of a clandestine campus free-love society) and together Tichnor and Shanks laid the groundwork for the
kind of experimental liberal arts college whose time, they
believed, had come.

They were prototype new-left liberals, and their
novel enterprise captured the attention, and the daugh-
ters, of like-minded wealthy gringos, many of them artists
and rich bohemians. That the school shaped up as a near-
conventional women's college, rather than a rats' nest of
free-love and communism, is testimony to the pair's
restraint and clear thinking. It was also a result of Miss
Tichnor's sudden death from peritonitis at the age of
seventy-eight, the very month that the college opened its
doors, and a result too of the subsequent sacking of the
visionary Shanks by the board of trustees when it was
discovered that he had been fobbing off with considerable
sums from the building fund and stupidly stashing it in
local Vermont banks.

His replacement, Dr. Bowman Beechcraft, was a
legit, albeit leftist-liberal, educator recruited out of the
University of Michigan. He made short work of some of
Tichnor's and Shanks's more outlandish innovations,
such as the resident abortionist who was to pose as
"college physician," the courses in Gurdjieff and
Ouspensky under the proposed "Department of Spiritual
Growth," and the observance of May Day as a Leninist
holiday (it irked the locals).

What kind of school did Reddington become, then?
While we pay homage to Tichnor for outflanking her
greedy relatives and the Bureau of Internal Revenue, in
the end her flaky vision was stymied and her will
abridged. Reddington turned into a fine arts college for
rich bitches. True, creativity was nurtured at the expense
of some order and decorum. But after his second year on
the job, Dr. Beechcraft once again foiled Tichnor's design
by introducing a grading system and cracking down on

the course requirements for the BA degree to ensure that Reddington's graduates would at least go out into the world knowing how to read, write and add up a column of figures, as well as paint nudes and play the viola. This move especially pleased the accreditation societies and impressed the more skeptical rich daddies of college-aged girls.

In other respects, though, President Beechcraft was loyal to the free-thinking sentiments he at least partly shared with the late Tichnor and her handpicked board of trustees. In parietal matters policy was unusually lenient, some said to the degree of licentiousness. Where other Yankee girls' colleges required their students in the dorms by 9:00 P.M. weeknights and midnight on weekends (some under lock and key!) the little darlings of Reddington had no party-pooping curfews to rebel against. They could steal off for weekends without letters of permission from home. They could have men in their rooms, as long as these visits didn't violate the peace of others. They could smoke cigarettes (pipes or Havana coronas if they preferred) anywhere on campus except the chapel. When Prohibition ended, they were allowed to keep booze in their rooms, under the sensible theory that they were better off getting blitzed on the premises than driving into ditches and trees.

In more recent times the same policy, or attitude, winked at the recreational use of drugs. Not that students were encouraged to smoke dope or drop mescaline. But unlike other colleges in the paranoid sixties, Reddington didn't hire informers or other low-down scum to spy on its student body. Nor did it cooperate with local "law enforcement" ninnies who slobbered over their Old Glory lapel-pins for a chance to stage a big campus crackdown raid. Nor did the college expel students nabbed for speeding—and subsequently found to be in possession of a "roach" or a single incriminating seed. In fact, in more than one case the college itself hired first-class attorneys when some local justice threatened to salt away a kid as "an example." In the tradition of its founder, Reddington College did not suffer the impertinence of vengeful rustic yo-yos.

From the beginning Reddington girls were among the most sought-after in New England. More randy young men passed through the tiny village train depot on Friday nights than at Vassar, Smith, Wellesley, and Sarah Lawrence combined. At Reddington a young man could linger in his sweetheart's dormitory boudoir without the screaming intrusion of a blue-haired housemother or other such senile killjoys. In the stillness of a cold Vermont night, little hearts beat warmly, like bees in cells of honey.

When Eleanor Hayes Tichnor set out to create the school, she didn't just donate a bunch of land. First of all, she bought half the town.

Reddington, Vermont, you see, is really two villages. First, there is New Reddington (now simply called Reddington), a typical USA Gringo Main Street village of brick shopfronts, car showrooms, Five and Ten stores, cinder-block pizzerias and squat supermarkets straddling Route 7, the main north-south artery on the western slope of the Green Mountains. Without Route 7, New Reddington (or simply Reddington) would not exist, in fact, did not exist, until the highway was created around the turn of the century.

Two miles away, on a shelf of mountainside overlooking New Reddington, is perched the village of Old Reddington (once known simply as Reddington, but no longer). This is the village originally settled in 1755 by the Bostonian Enoch Redding. In the beginning, it was a supply station for trappers on their way to the pelt-rich Adirondacks. Next, came the hordes of Eastern New

Englanders, tired of scratching out a living from the Bay State's stony, played-out soil, who passed through *Redding's Town* on their way to the more fertile western lands. Some of them marched no farther than this pleasant village above its peaceable valley. Soon a farming economy was established, its grains and beeves finding a ready market in that nearby boomtown, Albany.

In 1777 now-*General* Enoch Redding and his home-grown troops wiped up the floor with a regiment of Hessian mercenaries cut off by the fumbling retreat from Saratoga of the British General Charles Smythe. This massacre is immortalized in history as the Battle of Reddington, and today a marble obelisk maintained by the US Park Service commemorates the spot.

Old Reddington (or simply Reddington) then dropped off into a sleep from which it never fully recovered. It continued as the trading center for a small farming community. But burgeoning Yankee industry considered nearby North Adams, Mass., with its mighty Housatonic, a more attractive place to set up shop. The economy of Reddington remained focused on simple agriculture, and the population stabilized at about 1,000 souls. A whole century turned. With it came the motor car. With the motor car came Route 7. And with Route 7 came the village of *New* Reddington. Old Reddington's long coma came to an end. The tidy village perched on a mountainside above a peaceable valley was dead.

By the time the 1920's rolled around, and with them the eschatological ambitions of Eleanor Hayes Tichnor, a lively debate had erupted in New Reddington over what should be done with the abandoned, decaying village up on the mountain. There were civic ambiguities as to title and zoning, et cetera. The old village had turned almost overnight into a colossal white elephant. Now, it was a tax burden and a fire hazard.

It was also a place, a *thing*, of historical importance.

The hallowed battlefield comprised the old village commons, and located right smack dab in the center of it was
the government-maintained obelisk. It was agreed that
moving the obelisk down into the valley would not only
smack of opportunism, but would be a fraud on the
trickle of interested tourists, as well as on the descendants
of old Enoch, many of whom held civic posts of one sort
or another.

The debate smoldered for years until Eleanor Hayes
Tichnor stepped in to save the day.

Who was this sainted Eleanor, anyway?

Eleanor Hayes Tichnor's grandfather, Josiah Hayes,
was a prosperous China merchant of Salem, Mass. He
had climbed high enough up the ladder of plutocracy to
marry off his youngest daughter, Elizabeth, to the sought-
after Thomas Tichnor of the Boston clipper-ship building
Tichnor family. Thomas, for his part, branched out and
became one of America's leading designers of yachts—
Pierpont Morgan's *Egotist* and Carnegie's *Union Leader*
being only two to sail unfurled from his drawing board.
Thomas Tichnor was also something of a Utopian and a
late-blooming Transcendentalist. He inculcated in his
only child, our Eleanor, a belief in the Oversoul and the
sanctity of nature, to which metaphysical stew he added
dashes of Robert Owen and Amos Bronson Alcott, and
the aromatic free-love spice of Margaret Fuller. Eleanor
was clearly his favorite. Besides, there was no *other* except
Elizabeth, his wife, an invalid for years after childbirth,
then dead before the milestone of thirty summers. (Possibly Eleanor's abhorrence of marriage had its seed in this
invalid mother—a reminder, for all Eleanor's devotion to
Papa Thomas, of how closely the tie that binds can come
to resemble the hangman's noose.)

In his grief Thomas came to Vermont. He purchased
a tract of fifteen hundred-odd acres from the dissolute

grandson of Enoch Redding and built a mansion fit to rear a daughter in. At age five, she was already reciting Shelley and Lord Byron, a precocity which scandalized the visiting grandparents. From these poets, he moved her along to sturdier American fare, Emerson and Thoreau, both of them house guests at different times. (An entry in Thomas Tichnor's journal for the year 1857 records an instance of misbehavior on the great Thoreau's part. While "raving at dinner" one evening of the two-story observatory he planned to build at Walden Pond, "Henry," the journal says, "stood upon his chair so as to show the heighth of his telescopic invention for scanning the heavens, and said chair giving way beneath him, proceeded to punish the dainty object by striking it repetedly [sic] with his foot!") A brass plaque in the chairman of the music department's office—formerly the dining room of the Tichnor mansion—commemorates the great man's visit, and those of other notables. And Thomas Tichnor's journals are available in the Reddington College library to anyone with the proper scholar's credentials.

The years went by at *Elysium*, as Thomas named the estate, and Eleanor was now a young woman. After receiving an art education at Paris and Florence, she returned home to care for her Papa, now an invalid himself from a paralytic stroke. He regained sufficient use of his right hand to resume designing yachts. But, unable to ramble the grounds and nearby woods without assistance, he seemed to lose his former verve for life. In his final years, he refused to dress except in the merest rags, like Tolstoy ashamed of his aristocratic birth. When he died, in 1880, he left a fortune. It all devolved on Eleanor.

Never a sentimentalist, she observed a suitable period of mourning. Then suddenly, on the very doorsill of old-maidhood, Eleanor commenced to blossom. Seeking succor in the philosophies of her youth, she established a Utopian community at *Elysium* along the lines of Alcott's earlier model.

For thirteen years the communards grew their own vegetables, play-acted the Greek myths outdoors on warm summer evenings with daisy-chains in their hair, and fornicated discreetly in the woods, fields and thickets. Thirty-five adults and a dozen children lived that way at *Elysium* in its days of glory. They kept to themselves and avoided any flamboyant display which might rouse the ire of the simpler locals.

Then, in 1893, the enterprise was scuttled when a scoundrel named Clarence Gillette announced that he was Christ incarnate and lured away three-quarters of the members to the New Jerusalem he envisioned on the banks of the Willamette River in Oregon.

Gillette failed miserably. But when a handful of apostates crawled back to Vermont three years later, all they found was a now gray-haired Eleanor with no commune, a renewed ardor for the aristocratic life, and a rabid hatred for back-stabbing, born-again Christians. Gone were the vegetable gardens and the Grecian frolics. *Elysium* was once again a bucolic artist's salon, where Eleanor wined and dined the luminaries of her day, herself practicing the art of conversation with William Howells, Samuel Clemens, Henry Adams, Winslow Homer and a host of others, including the fiery young Stephen Crane.

She kept it up for more than a decade, until the death of Clemens, or "Dearest Sammy" as she called him. The tragic death at twenty-nine of the beautiful Crane in London some years earlier, had already jolted her to a degree that caused her to wonder if she had any more stomach for great literature than she had had for the Utopian life. Anyway, she was now a mere batty old lady alone with her memories.

She spent the better part of the years 1910-1920 awaiting that final, sickening slide into senility which never came. Then, tired of waiting, she rose again like a Phoenix with that web of schemes and ambitions which culminated in Reddington College.

Elysium directly adjoined the northern edge of Old Reddington village. Though she lived in virtual seclusion, somehow Eleanor caught wind of New Reddington's plight, and showed up, to the awe of most present, and the titters of a few, at a meeting of the town board when debate over what to do about the old village was at its hottest.

Imagine the scene.

She strode into the town hall in a yellowed gown decades out of fashion, her nose pointed aristocratically ceilingward, her lower lip curled in an apparent sneer (actually the result of a minor stroke), and announced that she was prepared to buy the ghost town on the mountain-side lock, stock, and barrel, if the village fathers would only name their price.

There was excited murmuring in the galleries. The mayor, a short, stout, florid-faced optometrist (and a Redding), huddled on the rostrum with the presidents of the Rotary and Kiwanis clubs and the head of the local Grange. After a few minutes the mayor announced that they would need some time to think about it.

Eleanor replied that she wasn't of a mind to waste precious time, nor come to another of their smoky and smelly meetings. The murmuring in the galleries grew fervid, and a little indignant. The village fathers huddled again. The mayor banged his gavel and, fighting a coughing spasm, suggested a figure of $250,000. His eyes darted wildly in their sockets. Eleanor let him have it.

"If you think I'm going to pay a quarter of a million dollars for that rattletrap collection of stovewood, broken

windows, stray cats, cobwebs and fallen plaster, then you
are out of your minds."

"Don't forget the monument, ma'am," the mayor
added.

"Yes, there's the monument," the Kiwanis president
insisted.

"President Harding will see to the monument, thank
you," Eleanor told them. "I'm offering you gentlemen
one hundred thousand dollars and not a penny more."

"But . . . But . . . But—"

"Take it or leave it."

The village fathers huddled once again. Eleanor grew
visibly impatient. Some feared she might walk out. There
were cries from all quarters of the gallery: "Take it!" The
red-faced mayor wheeled abruptly.

"We'll take it!" he cried, and cheers filled the hall.

"Very well," Eleanor said, a weary smile visible on
one side of her palsied mouth. "My attorney shall send
you a check in the morning. Good night, gentlemen."

And her business thus concluded, Eleanor left.

Workmen were soon brought in to transform Old
Reddington's thirty-odd (some of them very odd) buildings into the core of a modern college campus. The old
Redding Hotel, a brick structure of vaguely Georgian
design and the largest of the lot, was gutted and made
into a dormitory. Other ramshackle, weather-beaten
buildings, many of them the former homes of tradesmen,
were put to similar use. The empty shopfronts along the
village commons were converted into classrooms, labora-
tories, offices and studios. The abandoned Episcopal
church on the north side of the square was desanctified
and transformed into a student union and social center,
and a new wing was added to house a gymnasium
(Eleanor was a strong believer in physical fitness). The
broken-down opera house was logically restored for use
as a theatre.

When the work was done (and nobody knew for sure how much it finally cost, though estimates run as high as five million dollars), Eleanor appeared one day at the foot of the obelisk with President Shanks at her side, waved her cane menacingly at the assembled workmen, and then at the spanking restoration all around them, and croaked in her bone-brittle voice, "I guess it'll have to do."

Eleanor turned out to be even more ahead of her time than she realized. The place looked like Disneyland. It was so appealing that she could have charged admission to get in. And that is precisely what she did. She charged a bundle for tuition. The college was born. In a month's time, Eleanor Hayes Tichnor was dead.

Over the next fifty years Reddington College underwent a continuing process of expansion, annexation, land-grabbing and building. As the student body grew from the initial seventy-eight–member class of 1927, more classroom and dormitory space had to be added. In the 1950s the "cluster-concept" of student housing was introduced. This simply meant that small, self-governing minidorms were created on new property and incorporated, wherever possible, around existing buildings— farmhouses, barns, mansions, what-have-you. Clever architects were engaged to design complementary structural additions. These clusters were then designated as the "Farmhouse Cluster," the "Barn Cluster," the "Granary Cluster," and so on, consistent with their appearance. Where redundancy threatened, the clusters were named after birds. A provision in Eleanor Hayes Tichnor's will prohibited the naming of buildings after human beings, living or dead.

The housing concept seemed very avant-garde in the fifties. But, in reality, the dorms functioned a lot like sorority houses, with rushing and associated nastiness. There was snobism.

Also, over the years, these units developed nick-names. The original dorms along the old commons were dubbed "Society Row" and appealed to the debutante types. The restored Redding Hotel became known as "The Chelsea" and attracted the bohemian intellectuals. The old mansions on the street behind it were called "Luxury Row" and were claimed by art students, who liked the spacious, well-lighted rooms for painting. "Blue-jay House" way off in the woods was disparagingly referred to as "Siberia" in the early years, but later took on the more enchanting moniker "Xanadu" when LSD arrived on the scene and isolation became an advantage.

Last, but not least, the old Tichnor mansion itself, the heart and soul of old *Elysium*, was converted to house the department of music. This is especially ironic, because for all her talents, energy and brains, Eleanor Hayes Tichnor was completely tone-deaf and was known to despise the sound of music as others despise the shrieking of crows.

And now I shall also tell you what I think that mysterious scent of sea-water really was. It took me more than a year to figure it out. It was the smell of hormones.

four

A "nice, relaxing weekend in the country."

These, you will recall, were the words used by Dr. Bernard ("call me *Bud*") Royce to describe my "orientation" visit the weekend before the Fourth of July. It turned out considerably stranger than his words suggest. People say things, and you take them at face value.

"We're going to Reddington for a nice, relaxing weekend in the country," I told Sally.

Just for starters, Dr. Royce was drunk from the moment we arrived. Not falling-down, puke-in-your-shoes drunk, but obviously shitfaced.

Put two different people in the same anxiety-provoking social situation and they will behave differently. Let's say you go to a party and you end up standing next to a guy who had his nose shot off in Vietnam. Any number of reactions are possible. One person might tell the guy how delighted they are to meet him and then run like hell for the bar. Me, I'd probably just stand there and try to talk about the Red Sox or something and quietly freak out.

Now, take Sally. If she found herself at a party standing next to a guy with no nose, the first thing she'd do would be to bring it to his attention. Then, she'd probably ask all the grisly details as to how he happened to get it shot off.

Not that she was a blundering oaf, you understand. She just couldn't restrain her native curiosity. Similarly, she had a hard time resisting the temptation to make her *true thoughts and feelings* known, even if they are better left to lie like sleeping dogs. One particular incident springs to mind. It was way back in our undergraduate days in Washington, late one night at the tail end of one of those beer-swilling parties the English department threw for visiting writers. Sally was talking to one of my professors out on the rear porch, where the kegs were. I was on my way out the screen door for a refill when I happened to overhear this gem: "You know, Rich says you're a real asshole, but I think you're fascinating!" Unbelievable!

What brought on these incredible lapses? Sheer perversity? I don't know. In my more lucid moments, I like to think that it was just an irrepressible desire to fuck things up. No other explanation suffices.

She also liked to pick fights, and for the same reason, I think. It was a sport with her, like fencing, and it required a great deal of charm to pull off without inviting evil consequences. She also happened to be quite attractive, physically, which, let's face it, can be a real advantage. After she told that professor that I thought he was an asshole, she went on to observe that *she* thought he was "sexy." This, she said to Dr. Marvin Kronenberg of George Washington University, the closest thing on two legs to an actual troll to be found between the Blue Ridge Mountains and Chesapeake Bay. Maybe she was drunk that night and especially reckless. I was pretty gone myself. But one thing I'm fairly certain about: the only part of Marvin Kronenberg that Sally wanted to fuck was his mind.

Anyway, she could make me very nervous in social situations and that first weekend at Reddington tested a considerable portion of the trust that remained between us. She was a willful girl, and later I shall tell you how she got that way.

But, getting back to that first weekend, I could tell after thirty seconds that there was going to be Trouble in River City. It started right on Dr. Royce's doorstep.

We were all standing at his front door, saying "Hi" and chit-chatting about the drive from Cambridge. That is to say, he and I were chatting and shaking hands. Then, suddenly, as if he only just discovered Sally standing beside me, Dr. Royce cried, "You must be Richard's wife!"

Sally agreed that this was substantially so.

"What a pleasure to meet you," she added. Her tone of voice was about as warm as the wind that blows across Hudson Bay in January. Dr. Royce, though, was too far gone to notice it. Instead, he took her hand and kissed it noisily, a loud slushy sound. I could see Sally wince. Dr. Royce concluded the antic gesture by pecking a series of short staccato kisses up her bare forearm before letting go.

"The pleasure is all mine," he said.

"My name is Sally. I don't believe I caught yours . . ."

"Uh, this is Dr. Royce," I stupidly explained. "The Chairman of—"

"The heck with this Dr. Royce stuff. Call me Bud," he said, a warm, oblivious smile on his lips beneath the bushy gray moustache he wore with the ends waxed and teased upward. He was a very tall man, probably six foot four, but stooped, as if he were losing a lifelong struggle with gravity.

A woman appeared in the open doorway, so slowly and quietly that she might have been an apparition congealing out of a mist. She was as tall as Sally, who's a big girl, but this woman couldn't have weighed ninety pounds. Dr. Royce saw me notice her and quickly introduced her as his wife, Peggy. It seemed to tax her energy just to say hello, and it occurred to me that she was possibly very sick. You could see her hip bones protruding against the fabric of her slacks. Her black hair was obviously dyed and looked uncombed, as if she had just gotten out of bed.

Dr. Royce slapped a mosquito on the back of his neck, invited us inside, and asked us what we were drinking. Sally said gin and tonic. I said Scotch.

"That's my boy," he said, slapping me on the back. He poured a drink that must have been four fingers high in a tumbler as wide as a mason jar. I knocked about half of it down in a couple of swallows.

After those first turbulent moments things seemed to settle down for a while. The house was a small, and very old, example of the Federal style. The ceilings were low and a fireplace in the living room had been restored to show the original baking ovens to the side. It suggested that the room had been a kitchen long ago. When I asked him the history of the house, Dr. Royce explained that it had been the original farmstead of Samuel Redding, youngest brother of the patriot Enoch, and he went on to offer what I thought was a pretty absorbing discourse on the history of Reddington itself. You could tell by listening to him that his classes must have been popular, and I hoped that Sally might just be open-minded enough to overlook those strange moments of introduction and find him likeable.

Meanwhile, a television was playing in the background with the volume turned down low. They were broadcasting highlights of that day's Watergate testimony. Maurice Stans, the Nixon campaign treasurer, was getting it up the ass from Senator Weicker. Peggy sat in a wing chair, bathed in the set's blue luminescence, isolated and ethereal, like a figure drowning in moonlight.

"Don't you love it?" I remarked.

"Pardon me . . .?" Dr. Royce said.

"The hearings."

"Oh," he said. He turned his attention to the set, watched the proceedings silently for a moment, then muttered, "Oh deardeardeardeardear . . ."

"What . . .?" Peggy said, as if she had just snapped out of a dream. Dr. Royce waved his hand at her, as if to annul the transaction. He got up, swirling his ice cubes and poured himself another drink. "Would you care for a refresher, Richard? Sally?"

"No thank you," we both said.

"In a while, maybe," I added.

"To tell you the truth, I find these hearings . . . rather disagreeable."

"Oh, yes, well, that's what I mean," I said stupidly.

"I hate to admit it, but I voted for that man."

"For Nixon?"

Sally made a little face, but refrained from commenting.

"Oh . . .?" I said.

Dr. Royce sighed and, looking down into his glass, said, "May God forgive me."

"What possessed you?" Sally inquired, in her modulated social-worker voice, dripping with clinical objectivity.

"Well, you couldn't very well vote for Mr. McGovern, now, could you?" Dr. Royce said and returned to his place on the sofa. "After the Eagleton thing?"

"We did," Sally said. "We voted for him in the only state he carried: Massachusetts."

"Don't forget the District of Columbia, Sal," I said.

"The District of Columbia," Sally retorted cheerfully, "is not a state, Richie."

"I know it's not a state. But it is an electoral entity."

"Okay then, we voted for McGovern in one of the two 'electoral entities' that he carried."

"There are elements about this Nixon thing that you young people may not understand," Dr. Royce said.

"About Watergate?" Sally said.

"No, no, no, no. About why so many of us voted for him," Dr. Royce said, and sighed lugubriously. "Of course we always hated him, from the very beginning, before he was even vice-president. For my own part I think I believed that only a retrograde Republican could get us out of Johnson's war, just as only a retrograde Republican could change our stupid policy toward China. I'm quite sure that Hubert Humphrey wouldn't have stopped the war, though I voted for him in '68. Bobby might have, but . . . well, it's not that I had any admiration for the man, but after the China thing one came to view Nixon as a strong, purposeful president, skillful in the international arena, despite his personal clumsiness. I don't think Hubert would have done as much. Next to him, McGovern . . . I just couldn't vote for the man. He seemed so peevish. Such an amateur. I sound like I'm apologizing for . . . well, I guess I am. Now: this," he concluded and gestured toward the screen. Stans was squirming in the witness chair. "I guess blood *will* tell, as Faulkner said."

"And he didn't end the war," Sally added, as if it was a hot flash.

"No," Dr. Royce agreed. "And my guess is that he'll be banging out license plates in the Leavenworth Stockade before this thing is over." A big smile lit up his face, his eyes crinkling almost shut and the waxed tips of his moustache making him look like a sort of patrician Santa Claus. He hoisted his glass. "Well, here's to Senator Ervin!"

We toasted America's favorite Country Lawyer. Peggy, I noticed, was not drinking. She smiled weakly and hoisted an empty hand, then retreated to that inscrutable private center of things, where perhaps her illness resided.

After that, the conversation took a less baleful turn. Dr. Royce told us about his two sons. One was a senior at Princeton. The other he described in a jocular, affectionate way as "a no-account drop-out banging nails in Colorado and living in sin with two women, neither one his lawful wife." Soon the subject turned to the courses I was going to be teaching, and I offered Dr. Royce a few ideas of my own. He said a seminar on the contemporary novel sounded "good." Then, he drained his glass, slapped his knee dramatically and announced that it was time to get on with the evening's agenda. First, he was going to show us our new house—the house supplied by the college as part of my salary arrangement. Then, he said, there was a "small affair" at "Mac" MacWhorter's house, "just a down-home-Vermont-style-bar-be-cue-and-meet-the-folks," Dr. Royce said.

While we waited at the door, he kissed his wife dryly on the cheek. She said, "goodnight," and floated upstairs as if propelled by a current of air.

"Isn't Peggy coming?" I asked, regretting it at once.

"She isn't feeling very well," Dr. Royce said quietly and with a sigh. Then, with an abrupt about-face and in a voice ringing with attempted good cheer, he announced that there were only "three thousand drinking hours left until Christmas."

When I saw how unsteady he was on his feet, I offered to be chauffeur for the evening and he did not object in the least.

Our new home was a 150-year-old farmhouse in a wooded glade between the Granary dormitory and Blue-jay House in a rather remote corner of the campus proper. It was a small house, but in every way the incarnation of

ـhat simple, honest Country dwelling that had loomed for so long at the center of our sappy Country dream.

Dr. Royce threw on a light. An antique woodstove stood on iron paws in a corner of the living room. Its isinglass window was intact, and a box of splints nearby indicated that it was in working order. At the other end of the room was a working fireplace. Upstairs there were only two bedrooms and a bath. The kitchen, downstairs, had butcher block countertops, a new gas range, a marble pastry slab, and one of those French wrought-iron pot hangers suspended from the ceiling. I could see Sally's eyes light up as she moved around, running her hands across the marble and wood surfaces. It was a far cry from our kitchen hearth in Cambridge with its intruding dressers, its roach-infested Congoleum, and its three-burner electric range with a busted oven. The house was partly furnished with pieces of Shaker furniture in the Country mode. I put my arm around Sally's waist, and she rubbed her hand up and down my back. Then, Dr. Royce ruined it with a surprise:

"Of course, you lovebirds are prepared to be on-call once a month?" He sort of tossed it off, as an afterthought.

"On-call?" Sally wondered out loud.

"Didn't I mention it? It's nothing really. It's just that our students don't have dorm-mothers or supervisors, you know, so the way we work it here is that the younger faculty members who live on-campus take turns being on-call. In case of an emergency. It's no big thing. Didn't I mention it to you, Richard?"

"I don't remember anything about it, sir."

"Oh. Hmmmm. I must have assumed Dean Lansing informed you then."

"He didn't, as far as I recall."

"No? Oh my . . . well, it's nothing, believe me—"

"How often are we supposed to be on-call?" Sally inquired.

"Oh, just one weekend a month. That's all. I'm terribly sorry I forgot to tell you," Dr. Royce said. He may have been sobering up because he seemed to be picking up on Sally's chagrin.

"I didn't know that babysitting was part of the arrangement," Sally said pleasantly. I felt like clamping my hand over her mouth, alarmed at what might come out next.

"Believe me, dear," Dr. Royce assured her, "it's no big deal, strictly a parietal formality. We did it ourselves, Peggy and I, our first two years here, and would you believe we didn't get a single call? The way it works, you see, we give the little darlings your phone number in case somebody's on a bad LSD trip or some emergency crops up. But no one ever calls. Once, Bob Krock—you'll meet him later at Mac's—once, I believe, Bobby got a call. One little call in two years. A girl wanted to borrow his jumper-cables. It's nothing, believe me."

"You'd have to stay around the house, wouldn't you?" Sally said. "When you're on-call?"

"Oh, yes and no. I mean, you're supposed to, officially, but no one ever does. Just leave some number where you can be reached."

"But what if you want to go skiing or something. Or just go out for a walk?"

"Then . . . you just go," Dr. Royce said with a smile, adding, "and pray that some bubblehead of a freshman doesn't take an overdose until you get back."

"Great. . . ." Sally said, mainly to herself, but with a histrionic roll of the eyes.

"Believe me, please," Dr. Royce tried once more to reassure her, "the whole thing is a big nothing. It may sound a little onerous, but it's a joke to all of us who've been through it. So let's not have any more grousing, my dears. Now, what do you say we get over to Mac's before they send the state troopers out to look for us."

Dr. Royce killed the lights and walked out ahead of us to the car.

"Why are you being so difficult tonight?" I asked Sally in the dooryard when the old fellow was out of earshot.

"Who's being difficult?" she replied.

"You're being very contrary for some reason."

"Who's being contrary?"

"Okay, okay, I'm sorry I mentioned it. But for Pete's sake, Sal, give people a chance, huh?"

"You know how I feel about juice-heads, Richie."

I took her hands.

"I know how you feel, darling. But these are just little social obligations. We don't have to spend the rest of our life with this guy."

"God, I hope not."

"Don't worry," I told her and kissed her fingertips.

"It's a beautiful house, Richie."

"Come on, let's go."

Along the same lines as taking care not to inflict unkindness on poor schmucky people, or people with obvious deformities, I also hesitate to arrive at snap judgments of people's character. I find first impressions unreliable. As you may have noticed, this was not exactly the case for Sally, who could tell whether she loved somebody or hated their guts after about thirty seconds of unbiased observation.

Not that I don't stereotype people or pigeon-hole them myself. To some degree it's unavoidable, right? You see some guy playing tennis in black socks, or talking in some low-rent dialect, or driving a certain kind of car, and your mind makes involuntary leaps. But you don't have to be a slave to your prejudices.

Sally's approach was more like the French system of jurisprudence: guilty until proven innocent. And I could understand her reaction to Bud Royce that first night. He was drunk, all right, and I wouldn't have appreciated that kissing business if I was in Sally's shoes. I just wished she could wait a little longer before passing sentence and broadcasting it to the world. It made me very nervous. And now, all of a sudden, we were about to plunge into a situation where, in one evening, we would meet most of the people who would comprise our social world for who knows how many years, people who would be our friends, or not, people we were going to be around all the time, maybe even a few genuine assholes. But, as we drove out of the campus gates that summer evening, I was really worried.

Michael "Mac" MacWhorter's house was an ultra-modern and impressive dwelling, a massive sculpture of natural wood planes, turrets, and bands of glass that looked as handsome in its surrounding parcel of woods as it might have looked amid the windswept dunes of Easthampton, or in the back pages of the *New York Times Sunday Magazine*. Parking on the road in front of it, behind a dozen other cars, I tried to calculate its cost, and at today's inflated prices I'd figure it above $250,000. And I also wondered about the singular nature of its owner. I remembered being introduced to him a few weeks earlier, at the time of my interview, but in my memory he was just a name with no face attached. I was vaguely aware of his reputation in poetry circles—not as a poet himself, but as editor of a highly regarded "little" magazine, the *Reddington Review*.

Dr. Royce didn't trouble himself to ring the doorbell.

He just walked in and led us through the living room to a
wide rear deck where perhaps thirty people were standing and sitting, drinks in hand, in the soft, flickering
yellow glow of the bug torches. Electric floodlamps
concealed beneath the raised deck beamed silvery light
into the woods, a theatrical kind of light, brilliant and
vivid, as if the man who could afford such a beautiful
house might also hire an acting troupe to perform *A
Midsummer Night's Dream* in his backyard for the pleasure
of his guests. A child, a boy perhaps three years old, was
playing with a toy truck near the edge of the deck. He
repeatedly rammed the truck into the side of a redwood
planter. Classical music was playing above the deck
through high-quality speakers that did not distort the
sound. It was baroque, Handel or Telemann or somebody.

"Ah, so here's our youngest Turk and his lovely wife,
his very lovely wife," a voice said and I turned to my
right.

"Hi, Mac. Lovely night," Dr. Royce said.

"Bud," our host said dryly to Dr. Royce, with a
rather perfunctory nod of the head, I thought. "Splendid
weather, all right. Splendid evening. And splendid company, I hope, for our new colleague and his lady. I'm so
glad you could come."

He held out his hand and I shook it and so did Sally.
He was a wirey man, about forty I guessed, with gray hair
very carefully cut and combed and a full salt-and-pepper
beard, also carefully groomed. His face was cheerfully
rugged, with a fine, slightly upturned Celtic nose, a
generous smile, and lustrous, even teeth. His eyes were
entirely free of lines, but he wore glasses. The frames
were dark tortoise-shell. I would describe him altogether
as an exceptionally good-looking man, except his costume
was so strange.

He was wearing battered old tennis shoes with holes on the side that revealed his toes, Bermuda shorts in a green-and-red tartan pattern, a pink oxford dress shirt, and a scarlet ascot. I could see Sally staring at it.

Mac asked us what we were drinking and we told him. He sent his wife, Cleo, to a makeshift bar that had been set up at the far end of the deck. She was a handsome woman herself, also probably around forty, but coming to her early middle-age like a young actress in a college play, in a role far beyond her true years—the hair is dusted gray, while the face remains implausibly fresh and the body trim, with all the curves in the right place. Also, she was dressed in a very sexy outfit, a black leotard top and a floor-length cotton skirt with a rainbow printed on the fabric. She had a husky, appealing voice.

As for the other men, and their wives, who made a circle around us to say hello, I recognized a few faces as members of the English faculty, but the rest were strangers. Among them was the famous Bob Krock, famous not only for being the only person who ever got a call when he was on-call, but also as a distinguished young American poet with a growing reputation. I had seen a volume of his poetry as far back as the Columbia days, but to tell you the truth, I did not remember anything about it, except that I rather liked it. He was a short, stocky, powerful-looking guy about five-seven, probably in his late thirties. His complexion was olive-colored, his hair was black and his eyes were very dark brown. He looked a lot like those photos of the youthful Jack Kerouac, even to the degree that he seemed like a creature from another decade, another era, the fifties. His black hair had a slightly greasy, tousled look, and a little more artful comb-work might have turned it into a duck-tail. As it was, it just looked windblown, though there wasn't a breath of a breeze on the deck. If he hadn't said a word, you might have pegged him for an Italian, but the fact was he spoke with a conspicuous Southern accent. He was a Baptist from North Carolina.

His wife, Annie, oddly enough, was a Long Islander from Huntington, only a few miles from my own home-town of Oyster Bay, and when we discovered that, we spent several minutes playing the *do-you-know . . . ?* game, until it was established that we didn't share a single home-town acquaintance. She was a big-boned, athletic-looking woman with sandy hair and freckles and a sunny disposition that you noticed immediately. Both of them were dressed in simple, unassuming polo shirts and jeans and I liked them both at once.

In a little while, we ceased to be the center of attention. Somebody had changed the records and put on José Feliciano. A moment later, Mac emerged from the sliding glass doors with an enormous platter of steaks. He was now wearing one of those barbecue aprons with cartoons and snappy jokes printed on it, and motioned with his head for me to follow him over to the built-in grill. Sally was right behind, and tagging along with her was Bud. He was beginning to look unsteady on his feet again.

"Did you show the Turk his new quarters, Bud?"

"Sure did, Mac."

"What do you think?" Mac asked. He impaled his steaks, one at a time, on a big fork and laid them carefully on the grill over the coals.

"It's a real nice house," I said, and Sally agreed.

"We calls it 'Slavery Row,'" Mac said with a big grin.

"I beg your pardon. . . ."

"Oh, do-Lawd! Dat's what dey calls it, chile," Mac elaborated. To make sure we got it, he added a few steps of the Black Bottom and rolled his eyes around in their sockets.

Now, to me it was no big deal; in fact, I thought it

was kind of funny. But one thing that Sally just could not stand was racial jokes, and I shuddered a little to imagine what she was thinking. As you know, she had been a social worker. Fortunately, though, Sally didn't say anything. She just used the opportunity to glug down her drink. Unfortunately, Mac seemed to think he was mining a regular mother-lode of comedy and didn't stop there.

"De reason dey calls it Slavery Row am because y'all gots to be on de beck an' call ob de white chilluns in de big house."

He suddenly changed his tone of voice to falsetto to signify *white girl* and pantomimed talking into a phone:

"Oh, Jandy, I would appreciate it ever so much if you brought a couple of juleps up to my room right away. And did you remember to iron my gown for the cotillion?"

Back to the other voice:

"Yass ma'am, Ah sho nuff did, sho nuff."

Falsetto again:

"Why, thank you, Jandy—oh yes, would you please be so kind as to pluck a gardenia for my hair on your way over with those juleps."

Once again the "black" voice:

"Sho nuff, ma'am! Yass ma'am! Nuffin Ah likes better den pluckin' flowers fo' yo' sweet golden head, honeychile!"

By this time, just about everybody in the vicinity, including Mac himself, was at least tittering—except Sally, of course, who was literally hiding behind her drink. I also noticed that Bob Krock was staring down at the deck, barely grinning, and swirling the ice around in his glass.

"Now, just a second, Mac," Bud said, wiping a little moisture from the corner of his eye, "you're going to give these two nice young people the wrong impression about us."

"Am I?" Mac said. "Oh Lawdy, Lawdy, Ah's sho nuff sorry, Massa. Please Massa, please, don' whip me again! Please, Massa, hab mercy. . . ." And with this, Mac suddenly began bowing and scraping at the Chairman's feet, barbecue fork still in hand. This antic seemed to evoke less laughter from the crowd. As it died down, Sally could be heard clearing her throat. I closed my eyes.

"I've already gotten quite an impression," she said. "And for your information, I don't think it's particularly clever or amusing to make fun of black people."

Try to imagine the pall that this Statement of Principle cast over the gathering, or how much I wished I could melt through the planks of Mac's deck like a glob of Silly Putty and just disappear. I might add in Sally's defense that she was entirely sincere. Even during our darkest days in Harlem, after a rip-off, or some ghastly street scene, Sally would refute and condemn my racial slurs. In other spheres, Sally was not always such a model of rectitude, as you will see. But in this department she was definitely for real.

I don't know how long that horrible interval of silence lasted. All I remember is the sound of steaks sizzling, and watching everybody look in any direction except at Sally or Mac or me. But, finally, it was Mac himself who smoothed things over with the skill of an experienced diplomat.

"No," he said, "I wouldn't want you nice young folks to get the wrong impression about us. After all, we're really nice folks too, at heart, when you get to know us better. I think you'll find the society here a whole lot better than my regrettable performance might indicate."

His tone of voice in this was also sincere, dignified, and without sarcasm. You could feel the tension begin to evaporate. A few people on the sidelines even nodded their heads in agreement. Then Mac added, "We're all really card-carrying liberals here—except Krock over there, who's a member in good standing of the Ku Klux Klan."

Once again there was the sound of laughter, and even a smattering of applause as Krock lifted his arms and made the Nixonian V sign with his fingers. The spell was over and I breathed easier.

"Hey, let me see your card, wise guy," Sally said with a sly smile to show there were really no hard feelings as long as she got her point across. And to show likewise, Mac draped an arm around Sally's shoulder and offered his other hand to shake in view of the assembled guests, who applauded when she took it. You got the feeling that you were watching two veteran ball-busters who had met their match and seemed to respect one another. You also got the feeling, diplomacy aside, that they already hated each other's guts.

"That's my girl," Mac told her with a squeeze, before he went back to his steaks. The hum of conversation resumed. Cleo went off to mix a fresh round of drinks.

The food was excellent—beautiful steaks, aged to perfection and as tender as could be. There was garlic bread, a spinach-and-avocado salad, stuffed mushrooms and baked potatoes. For dessert Cleo brought out a selection of cakes she had made. I tried them all, and they were superb, including a chocolate-whiskey cake that was as rich and good as anything from a fine New York bakery. One thing you certainly couldn't fault the MacWhorters on: they put out a magnificent spread. It also seemed to have a palliative effect on my paranoia. Or maybe it was the booze catching up. It seems, in my memory, that we did a hell of a lot of drinking that evening.

Around ten-thirty, Mac's doorbell started ringing like crazy and a whole new crew of people invaded the house. His parties, I would learn, were two-stage affairs—like those White House receptions for foreign dignitaries. The first stage, cocktails and a fine meal, was limited to a select circle of cronies and honored guests. Then later, he would throw open his house to the lesser fish, including students, of course. The second invasion had obviously begun, though not too many of the new arrivals were students because we were between sessions. The music was louder. The Beatles *Revolver* album was playing. It had grown chilly out on the deck, and most of the people had headed inside, Sally among them. I remained on the deck, though, sitting next to an older woman as thickly made up as a geisha girl.

"Ach," she said emphatically, "alvays he hess to play dat musig so loud you can't hear yourself tink!"

Being half in the bag, I stupidly explained to her that *Revolver* was "one of the watershed albums of rock music," and tried to persuade her to enjoy it.

She looked at me as if I were crazy, then said, "Who are you, young man?"

I told her. When the name didn't ring a bell, I explained that I was the newest member of the English department. She did not seem very impressed, and her reaction certainly deflated some of my earlier feelings of self-importance. She pointed to the crowd on the other side of the sliding glass doors and said, "A bunch of drunken slubs." Then, she said goodnight, gathered up a purse and a kind of satiny black shawl, and left.

Which left me alone out there, or so I thought, until I heard a belch and turned to see Bob Krock reclining on a chaise, out of the light, looking up at the stars with a bottle of beer balanced on his belly. I was about to follow the older woman inside when his voice stopped me:

"Hey, you, new boy . . . !"

I turned around.

"Come on over and set a spell."

"I thought I'd just go see how Sal . . . how my wife was doing—"

"She can take care of herself. Ooooweeee, can she ever take care of herself. Look, there she is right now, talkin' to ole Fishlips."

"Fishlips . . . ?" I said, mainly to myself. You could, in fact, see Sally right behind the glass doors. She was talking to the very woman who had just excused herself from my company. The woman had a hand on Sally's arm and seemed to be speaking excitedly. Of course you could not hear what she was saying. Sally was nodding her head vigorously. The woman did have large, fleshy lips.

"Who is that old lady?" I asked Bob.

"That's Fishlips."

"Is she somebody's wife?"

Bob broke up, spraying beer all over himself and the chaise. I handed him a nearby napkin. It took a couple of minutes for him to calm down again.

"Could you imagine wakin' up next to *that*?" he said and cracked up all over again. It was a long, wheezing guffaw and it was infectious. Just hearing it made you laugh too.

"So, who *is* Fishlips?"

"Fishlips," Bob said, "is Fishlips." This evoked another minute of laughter from both of us, but finally Bob seemed to sense that he had milked it about dry. "Her name is Neda Nagy. She's chairman of the music department. And I'll tell you somethin' else: if you catch her pawin' your wife, you better watch out."

"Hey, come on, now. You're kidding me—"

"It ain't for nothin' that she's led the single life."

"Jeez," I said. Inside, I could see the woman shake hands with Sally and vanish into the crowd. Then Sally herself vanished.

"Care to join me in a smoke?" Bob asked.

I sort of waffled for a moment.

"She'll be all right," Bob said. "Follow me."

Before I could say "no" he got up from the chaise and leaped over the rail to the lawn below.

To tell you the truth, I wasn't all that interested in getting stoned, really. I was already burned to a crisp from drinking. The truth was, I just wanted to get to know him, and impress him as a regular guy, so I went along.

Bob said the dope was in his car, so we walked around the house to the front. Then Bob asked if I felt like getting away from Mac's for a little while and taking a ride. I said, "fine."

He pointed to an eight-year-old white Chevy sedan parked along the road among all the newer, more sensible European cars. It was pocked with rust-spots. The played-out suspension left it sitting unnaturally close to the ground. We got in. The interior somehow had the smell of another decade, musty but not unpleasant. Bob reached around to the back seat and grabbed a couple of beers.

"I like 'em warm. Hope you don't mind."

"I'm not much of a beer drinker," I said.

"It'll grow on you."

Bob popped both of them out the window and handed me one. Then he reached over to the glove compartment, where there was a Ziploc bag of weed, and dropped it on my lap.

"Would you roll us one?"

"I suppose I could manage."

He turned over the engine. It started easily, but once it got going you could hear the clatter of loose valves. The muffler was pretty beat too. He maneuvered the big boat-like vehicle from its space between a Saab and a Volkswagen, and we rolled down the winding country road.

"Your wife's pretty gutsy to stand up to Mac like she did," Bob said after a while.

"I don't know if *gutsy*'s the right word. She has this

problem with her mouth. Sometimes it doesn't stay shut when it should."

"That's a hell of a way to talk about your wife."

"It's a fact," I told him. "She's a little weird that way." The thought of her lecturing Mac still made me cringe.

"Well, *gutsy's* the right word, believe me. I'm a poet, and I should know, right?"

He paused as if waiting for me to agree with him, and eventually I did.

"And I know Mac," he continued. "Believe me, it's very useful to set your limits with him from the word 'go.' In case you don't know it, and you probably don't, that man is the Rasputin of Reddington College."

"Really?" I said, lamely. The conversation was already making me nervous. I took a couple of swallows from the can of warm beer. I also noticed that Bob had a tendency to slip out of his thick Southern accent into blander, more educated inflections, as if it required a certain amount of exertion to keep it up, or as if he saved it for special effect.

"Yes, really," Bob said. "This is one dangerous bird we got here. A real meat-eater. He is full of more schemes, grievances, plans, machinations and maneuvers than Cesare Borgia. Some people sort of remind me of musical instruments, you know? Take me, for example. I'm sort of a trombone. I can be loud and brassy, but I also have this mellow, undulant quality. Basically, though, I'm a pretty simple instrument. With Mac, on the other hand, what you got is more like one of those spooky ole church organs that's got about eight thousand stops and keys and pedals."

"What am I?"

Bob looked at me.

"I don't know yet," he said. "Maybe . . . maybe a flügelhorn."

"A flügelhorn! Thanks a lot."

"How are you coming with that J?"

"Maybe if you pulled over for a minute. It's kind of bumpy."

"You're lookin' more like a flügelhorn," he said and brought the car to a stop. I rolled a joint and gave it to him.

"Does this meet your approval?"

"It looks very serviceable," he said and then lit it.

"Just out of curiosity, and as long as you brought the subject up, what has Mac done to you?"

"Me?" Bob snorted, "Nothin'. And I intend to keep it that way. Why, we're closer than two slices of bread, me and Mac."

"If you guys are so close, then how come you drive around the countryside bad-mouthing him to strangers?"

Bob stared at me for a moment, then chuckled.

"That's an interesting question," he said. He took a hit off the J, slipped down in his seat, and exhaled deeply. "Let's just say that I can't stand the sucker's guts. But there are a few reasons that Mac doesn't mess with me. Number one is that he thinks poets have supernatural powers. And they do, in his case. They have the supernatural power to sustain that man in his profession. Hey, did you notice the outfit he had on tonight?"

"What? The ascot?"

"Uh-huh. What did you think?"

"I dunno. A little eccentric, I guess."

"That's almost the right word for it. *Fruit* would be exactly the right one. That man doesn't know from one moment to the next whether he's the Duke of Wellington or a two-bit Dayton, Ohio, golf hustler."

Bob handed me the joint and put the transmission back in gear. Soon we were rolling down the quiet road at a slow, undeliberate rate.

"The story of Mac MacWhorter is the tale of education gone mad," he said. "The nineteenth century with its leaps in the natural sciences gave us Dr. Frankenstein, right? Well, Dr. MacWhorter is education's gift to the twentieth. And like Frankenstein, the fuel for Mac's progress is ambition. He comes out of a midwestern land-grant diploma mill, because no proper Eastern school will have him, and heads for the sultry shores of California, where he bluffs his way to a master's degree—"

"We all do," I interrupted, "to some extent."

"Maybe. But, you see, his thesis is rejected and somehow he mysteriously contrives not only to get it reconsidered and accepted—the same damn piece of shit—but published too."

"On what?"

"He fakes an interview with Robert Frost."

"Come on! Fakes it?"

"No kiddin'. Fakes it, outright. And to show you how diabolical he is, Mac produces a tape-recording to back it up. It's him talkin' with a down-and-out Hollywood character actor he finds in a nursing home who's havin' trouble payin' his bill. Still, it's a pretty uncanny job. The script, of course, is furnished in advance."

"How do you know all this?"

"I know because I do my homework, my friend. Unlike some others. Okay then, Mac strives again for the Eastern imprimatur, but still no Ivy League school will touch him, so it's off to the University of Iowa and its famous writers' workshop."

"That's supposed to be a real good place."

"Well . . ."

"That's what I hear—"

"Please, this isn't nearly the end. Okay, Mac arrives at the workshop. Need I tell you that Mac's bein' there is sort of like lettin' the fox into the hen-house, as my people would say. His ambitions inflame him and he rockets to new heights of treachery. He is caught red-handed in the room of a young man who has gone on to become an important literary personage of our day, whose name I will refrain from draggin' through the mud here. Anyway, this personage catches Mac in the act of riflin' his desk, in the drawer of which there is a novel this boy has shed tears of blood over. Mac is neatly throttled for his trouble. But, crawling off to lick his wounds in the dark night of his perfidious soul, Mac has another brainstorm. Threatened with exposure for the bungled theft, this shameless polecat returns to the scene of the crime and negotiates a way out of it with the very personage who was his intended victim. Here's the deal: Mac will pay five thousand dollars for this personage to write a novel which Mac can submit as his dissertation. To recapitulate now, failing to steal a dissertation, Mac has paid to have one written for him.

"The personage falls for it—not because he lacks principle per se, though a case might be made for it—but because he's so broke he can't resist it. He's been livin' on lentils as long as he can remember and five thousand dollars is a lot of money. The money, meanwhile, is a drop in the bucket to Mac MacWhorter, who, through some ghastly cosmic error, happened to have been born rich. His grandfather was the inventor of a patented nozzle which is used in the pumping systems of all refrigerators. Can you beat that?

"Anyway, three months later a manuscript is delivered to Mac as per the agreement. It is barely up to par even as pornography. Also, the villain of the piece bears an uncanny resemblance to the patron who commissioned it—a prank that is evidently lost on Mac. But still, he can't submit this piece of shit and he knows it. Of course, he can't welsh on the deal either because the author demanded cash on the barrelhead and got it. So what does Mac do? He hires out again, naturally. He finds some third-rate New York detective writer to ghost a comprehensive revision.

"Again, this knave is blessed with blind luck. Not only is his dissertation accepted, but it is published and gets sold to the movies! Years later when the movie finally gets made—a turkey starring Tab Hunter and Ann-Margret—the ghostwriter starts litigation and Mac settles quietly out of court. The personage who wrote the original book, meanwhile, doesn't happen to see the movie (which has a different title) and never finds out about the deal until years later. And by the time he finds out that he too has been screwed out of considerable money, it's too late.

"This novel, incidentally, this work, this opus, is the last novel Mac MacWhorter will ever . . . *produce,* naturally, for the excellent and obvious reason that he didn't write it in the first place. Also, it leaves him with the problem of what he will do next, where does he go from here, those fires of ambition still flickering in his mangey heart. In desperation, he beats another path back to Academia. There are a few, brief, restless years at the University of Idaho at Coeur d'Alene, where he makes too many enemies too fast to gain tenure. Besides, Idaho is jerkwater, and the wine of Mac's ambition o'erflows its vessel, you might say. He lands in New York City.

"Through some miracle of social cybernetics, Mac insinuates himself on the poetry scene which surrounds Ginsberg and his associates. It is now the mid-sixties, a period of great creative upheaval. Mac finds a niche for himself as a middleman between the poets and the public. He starts off booking them for readings around the Northeast. Soon, though, he becomes a power to be reckoned with. In a few scant years, Mac MacWhorter has turned into the Sol Hurok of American poetry, booking his clients into major university lecture halls for fat fees.

"Lo and behold, Academia beckons again. Reddington College offers him a job. It's Mac's big chance to legitimize himself. It's not Harvard, of course, but it's not Idaho either. And as you know, it's not a question of money. In short, Mac accepts. He builds himself a house that turns the old-timers green with envy. He settles in, and practically overnight becomes Vermont's pasha of poetry. His magazine—*The Review*—becomes a major forum for poetry and criticism, its pages filled with the pellucid verses and hermeneutics of Mac's former clients, many of them now 'friends.' They are just as eager to perform on videotape, and over the years Mac's archive of recorded interviews with major poets gains reknown. His leadership in the field is finally beyond dispute, which is pretty good when you consider that he doesn't practice the art himself. And that is the story of how he got where he is today. And here he is. And here I am. And here we are."

Bob had pulled into the campus somewhere. We turned on a circular driveway and stopped before a refurbished stone barn, to which were attached newer, lower wings built of similar but lighter-colored stone. There were no other cars in the vicinity, and the only light that burned was an outdoor fixture over the main entrance.

"What is this place?" I asked.

"Granary," Bob said. "It's a dormitory."

A breeze blew through the windows of the car, carrying on it the smells of things I was not yet used to. Clover. Hay.

"Why are you telling me these things?"

"Just thought you'd be interested," Bob said and reached into the back for another beer.

"Where did you get your information?"

"Let's just say that one of the principals is . . . an acquaintance of mine."

"Who? The famous personage?"

"Could be."

"But you're not saying . . . ?"

"Nope."

"But I gather that's the other reason Mac stays out of your way."

"I suppose I'm in a position to, shall we say, create a whole heap of unpleasantness for that man."

"But you go to his house, drink with him, socialize."

"That's correct. I keep up appearances."

"Why bother? You could just ignore him."

"Uh-uh," Bob shook his head. "For the same reason that you don't ignore a rattlesnake when he crawls inside your house. You like to keep your eye on him, make sure he doesn't come too close or crawl in your boots when you're not lookin'."

"That's not what I'd do with a rattlesnake. I'd kill him. You don't try to coexist in a house with a rattlesnake."

"No, you don't. That's true."

"Then you'd kill him, right?"

"Well," Bob drawled, "I guess my analogy limps a little. In fact, it limps a whole lot. A poet with a load on is no poet at all, in my opinion. You want some?" he said and proffered the can of beer. My mouth was dry from the dope so I took a few swallows.

"Bob, are you recruiting?"

"Recruiting . . . ?"

"Is this some big faculty war: you against Mac?"

"I'd think it would be obvious to you, Mr. Harvard Shit-for-brains, that I'm telling you all this for your own good. Your little wife has already waved the red flag at the bull. You're already in trouble, and you don't even know it."

"Wait a minute. He apologized. He was a gentleman about it."

"You really think so?"

"That was my impression."

"Well, I guess he sold you."

"He seemed sincere—"

"Aw shit! Artifice! He may have acted like the soul of humility for half a minute, but there is no limit to his capacity for mischief or his appetite for vengeance. One thing you don't do is wound that man's pride and get away with it. He's like one of those rogue elephants they got over in Africa that can run around for years, decades, after you done them some wrong, and then one day they come along and find you sittin' under the ole banyan tree and . . . well, that's all she wrote, my friend."

For what seemed like a long time, but was probably no more than a minute, we sat there in the car without speaking. I believe we both felt the oppressiveness of the silence. It was Bob who ended it.

"If I may be frank," he said, "I have a problem. Or rather a friend of mine has got a problem. It's Bud Royce. Mac has got the squeeze on Bud Royce."

"Bud Royce is a friend of yours?"

"Yes."

"A close friend?"

"That's right. You find that hard to believe?"

"I wouldn't think you had much in common."

"Bud Royce is not the man he used to be. That drunk, burnt-out clown you met tonight is not the Bud Royce who brought me into the department. He's runnin' scared and he's comin' apart."

"What does Mac want from him?"

"Mac wants to be chairman of the department. Unfortunately for Mac, that position is already occupied by Bud, who is not only tenured, but until fairly recently enjoyed reasonable prospects for another decade of active professional life. Now, I'm not so sure."

"It's his wife who looks pretty grim, if you don't mind my saying so."

"She takes a lot of downers."

"Must take an awful lot."

"She's committin' suicide and she doesn't even know it. It breaks my heart. It really does. Come on, let's take a walk and stretch our legs."

He chugged down the beer and reached back for another one, the last one. We got out of the car. My legs were stiff, but it was the sensation in my head that bothered me more: a strange, nonspecific conviction of doom. The sensation rattled me to the degree that I felt compelled to speak, if only to take my mind off it.

"One thing," I asked him, "you know all this stuff about Mac's past, but you don't use it. How come?"

"I use it. Just him knowing I know what I know is usin' it." He leaned against the car and sucked on his lower lip for a minute thinking. "On the other hand," he said, "it's such old stuff that part of me wonders if anyone would believe it . . . or care if they did believe it."

"Then it's not something you really hold over his head, is it?"

"I don't really know. But neither does Mac. And that's sufficient, I guess. You know, the Chinese have this saying when a baby is born. They don't say, 'May your life be a bowl of cherries,' or 'May you grow up to be rich and famous.' They say, 'May you live in interesting times.' Well, what we got here, my friend, is interesting times, and I hope you enjoy it."

With that final declaration, Bob began strolling, or rather, weaving, down along the gravel drive which curved down to the big stone granary. Every few steps, he picked up a handful of pebbles and winged them, forcefully, at the lighting fixture over the building. The stones missed their mark but disturbed the birds roosting under the eaves. Or perhaps they were bats. It was hard to see in the meagre light.

"Aw, man," Bob said, drinking in a lungful of air, "I love this place an awful lot."

I must have chuckled or something. I thought he was being facetious.

"No, my friend, you'll see what I mean. It gets into your blood, Vermont. Listen. Isn't it peaceful?"

"Yes."

"There's so much damn Yankee Doodlin' goin' on everywhere else you can hardly hear yourself think. This stillness, this peace—that's Vermont. That's these mountains, and I love these mountains. Where I come from the land's as flat as a pancake. I do love it here."

"It's beautiful," I agreed. "It's what Sally and I have dreamed about for years and years."

"You and Sally, huh?" he said to himself, as if he was trying to comprehend us more vividly as a couple.

"It was our dream."

"I believe it," he said, then pointed to the building before us with an expansive gesture. "In about a week these dorms are gonna be crammed to the rafters with so much fresh young poontang it's gonna blow your eyeballs clean out of their sockets."

"Hey, we're both married," I said, instantly regretting it.

"You bet I'm married," Bob said. "But you may be assumin' a whole lot about me when you say that."

"I'm an asshole," I admitted. "I really am."

"Aw, no you're not. You're just new here, that's all. You'll see. You'll be just like a little kid in a candy store."

"No thanks. I love my wife. You've got to be crazy playing around with students."

"Who says I play around."

"Well, isn't . . . I assumed . . ."

"Boy, you are just about the most assumin'est fellow I ever met."

"I think I know what you mean. We both do. I'm just saying it's dangerous."

"Oh, but it is. It's shot through with perils. And

rewards. Like life itself. Come on, let's get out of here."

We walked back to the car and got in. The engine started with its spastic clatter of loose valves.

"Hey, you ever fish?"

"I've been," I said.

"What kind?"

"Of fish?"

"Yeah."

"I dunno. Bass. Pickerel. The usual."

"That's not real fishing."

"Funny, I thought it was."

"Trout. That's fishing. Do you know how to use a fly rod?"

"No."

"I see. Well, in case you don't know it, the trout fishing hereabouts is superb. Would you like to learn?"

"Sounds good."

"I'll conduct a tutorial on the subject, with you as my sole student. The fee will be two six-packs per session. That sound fair to you?"

"Fine."

"You bet. And there isn't a better teacher around. I'll admit, I'm a hell of a poet. No, I don't deny it. It's true. But in that realm I'm simply one virtuoso among others. On a halfway decent trout stream I'm a whole lot closer to what God is like."

He threw the gearshift into first and we headed back to Mac's house.

The party had wound down considerably by the time we got back. About a dozen people were sitting in the living room watching a videotape of Mac interviewing the poet Galway Kinnell on a big color console. Among them, and not looking particularly enthralled, was Sally.

Bud Royce greeted Bob and me noisily when we suddenly reappeared, but Mac just as energetically hushed Bud down, saying, "This is the best part of the tape. Would you please keep it down!"

"Sure, Mac. . . ."

I slid onto the couch next to Sally and slipped my hand into hers. It was cold and limp. She had a pouty little expression on her face that was a sure sign of trouble.

"Where've you been?" she whispered in my ear.

"Just went out for a while," I whispered back.

"I know *that.*"

"Just went out for a little walk with one of the guys on the faculty."

"Well, thanks a lot. Would you ask Dr. Royce to take us back now before I start to scream."

"There's no need to scream, hon."

"You haven't been here for over an hour."

"We're going, Sal. Just cool your jets."

I leaned over to Bud who was sitting behind our sofa and to my right. "Pssst, Bud. Sal and I are pretty tired. Would you mind taking us back now?" Bud nodded reassuringly and got up from his seat. So did we. So did Mac, when he saw we were about to leave.

"You're not going, are you?"

"Yes, Mac," Bud said. "Richard and Sally have had a long day. They drove all the way from Boston this afternoon and it's been a long evening—though not without its felicities," he hastened to add.

"Sure, I understand," Mac said, that congenial smile of his showing the even rows of white teeth. "This is only one of the finest tapes in the collection."

"I know, Mac," Bud said, "but they have had a long day. Come on kids."

"Okay, if you three don't have the stamina to pay your respects to one of America's leading poets, then nobody's going to twist your arm." Mac still smiled lambently and shared it with the others in the room, to show that he didn't mean to sound like a scold.

"Pay our respects? To a tape?" Sally said to me in an incredulous tone loud enough for everyone else to hear. Mac glared at us now from his seat. The generous smile had vanished. I noticed Bob Krock sedulously studying his fingernails.

"Toodle-oo kids," Mac said stiffly and turned his gaze back toward the two small figures on the TV screen, one of whom was himself. The others waved goodnight as we followed Bud out of the room. Before we were out the front door, I could hear Mac's slightly nasal voice again:

"Come on everybody. Pipe down. This part coming up is the greatest. . . ."

Bud showed us up to the guest bedroom on the second floor of his house and said goodnight. I could tell that Sally was still smoldering from the way she kicked off her shoes. I could have ignored it, but something told me that if we didn't deal with it tonight, Sally's behavior would turn lethally hostile for the rest of the weekend. So I decided to meet it head on.

"Still pissed, huh?"

"You bet I am."

She took off her jeans, folded them neatly, pounded them flat with her hand, then laid them over the back of a chair.

"Well, you can't have it both ways, Sal. If you want to be a liberated woman then you can't look to me to lean on in every social situation."

"You have such a smug look on your face."

"It's not intentional, Sal—"

"And that thing you do with your eyelids—fluttering them when you want to be patronizing—"

"Who's being patronizing! I'm just saying you can't have your cake and eat it too. You want to be an independent person? An adult? Fine. Then learn to cope like one. But don't blame me for not being there when you get tired of coping. Or bored with it."

Sally made a strangled little noise and rolled her eyes up at the ceiling. You could tell that she was just barely stifling an impulse to scream her head off. Then, she violently pulled off her LaCoste shirt and flung it at me. Finally, she ripped back the covers and got into bed with her back to me.

I slowly took off my clothes, knowing I had to apologize somehow, and not knowing how to do it. Eventually, I also got into bed and put my hand on her bare shoulder. She tried to shrug it off.

"I'm sorry, Sal."

She didn't reply. She just lay there, very stiff and tense, and I could hear her grinding her teeth.

"Do you hear me, Sal. I apologize."

"And that's supposed to make it better?"

"Yes."

Suddenly she rolled over with such force that it knocked me flat on my side of the bed. She was now looming over me.

"You can be such a pig sometimes it's unbelievable," she said.

I hoisted myself upright so we were face to face.

"I may be a pig, but you are one of the most touchy, hostile people I ever met."

"I am not hostile," she said, her voice raising. "You have absolutely no insight about what my situation might be like, *for me*! For you everything is abstract. This bullshit about—"

"Sally, for Godsake lower your voice—"

"This bullshit about being independent, being liberated, having my cake, you don't know what the hell you're talking about. You left me stranded with those assholes!"

"Sally, honey, we're going to be living here, don't you realize that?"

She slunk back down under the covers, the edge of the sheet gripped tightly over the lower half of her face.

"I'll die," she said.

"No you won't. Sally, honey, it's going to be beautiful. Please, believe me. We don't have to spend any time with those people if you don't want to. It'll be just like our dreams: a house just like we always wanted. You can have your garden, a real garden, not just a garden in your mind from reading the seed catalogs. You'll be able to do all the things you've wanted for so long."

She shifted back over to her side. I started stroking her hair, pushing it behind her ears.

"Can we leave tomorrow?"

"You want to leave tomorrow?"

"Yes."

"But we were invited for the weekend."

"I know. But we can cut it short. We can make an excuse."

"Well . . . I guess we can."

"Please, Rich."

"Okay. We'll go back tomorrow. I'll tell Dr. Royce . . . something."

Sally reached up and squeezed my hand.

"Thanks, Rich."

"I love you honey."

"I love you too. You know that. Did you sign the contract yet?"

"Yes. Certainly I did. Two weeks ago."

"Oh . . ."

"Why?"

"Nothing," she said. "Just . . . nothing."

*   *   *

Was I being unfair to Sally that night? Insensitive? A pig? Undoubtedly, to the degree that I failed to apprehend the true nature of Sally's predicament—i.e., that the job at Reddington was *my* job, and no matter how you cut it, Sally was coming along on *my* ride, *my* trip, *my* life, and no matter how independent either of us fancied her to be, she was still basically *a wife*. Of course she was a wife the whole time I was in graduate school too. But this was different now. Like our fuckhead notions about Country Life, our conception of marriage was headed for the serious testing stage.

Bud Royce seemed disappointed when we made our transparent excuses over breakfast and told him we had to return to Cambridge earlier than expected. We made up some cockamamie story about being present at the birth of a friend's baby, or something equally ridiculous. Bud didn't try to talk us out of it.

Peggy did not even come down for breakfast. Bud made the bacon and eggs himself, not that it's such a difficult thing to do, but at 10:00 in the morning he already had whiskey on his breath. He seemed shrouded in a cocoon of terrible sadness. Just being around him convinced me more and more how Sally was right—I didn't want to stick around there anymore either, at least not for the weekend in Bud Royce's house.

We helped with the dishes and a little while later he walked us out to the old Volvo. I cranked it up. We said goodbye until late summer, when Sally and I would be returning for good, to move in.

I backed down the driveway. Above, a pale, motionless figure watched us from a second-story window.

five

On the drive back to Cambridge we resolved to take off for a few weeks in August, to go somewhere and get our heads together before the big move.

Through the rest of July, then, Sally kept working at the Food Stamp office while I went out and got a job waiting on tables at the Orson Welles Restaurant on Mass Ave (where I got to be buddies with their overeducated dishwasher). The dough was amazingly good. I averaged $60 a night in tax-free tips.

By August 1st we had accumulated hundreds of dollars to blow on our trip—having my salary and the perquisite house to look forward to come September, and thus no money worries. We purchased a two-man tent designed for assaults on Mount McKinley and also an inflatable boat. Sally said farewell to her friends at the office. I served my last plate of brown rice and poached salmon. We turned off the refrigerator, left a note for the mailman, and lit out for the Maine wilderness.

For two weeks we lived like aborigines. We parked the Volvo in the ranger station lot and hiked seven miles through the woods and bogs of Baxter State Park to an uninhabited lake. The weather was unusually hot and we quit wearing clothes during the daylight hours. Our lovemaking reached exorbitant depths of primitivism. (Once, while casting for pickerel from the shore, I spied Sally squatting near our lunch fire, her abundant bosoms dangling perilously over the flames. I lost my head, dropped my rod in the sand, and jumped her on the spot. Another time, our bogside fuckery startled a browsing moose, who galloped off through the reeds and rushes with the very fires of mortality lighted in her watery eyes.)

It was a dreamlike time. When we talked about Reddington at all, it was not about the geeks on the faculty, but of the farmhouse and Sally's plans for making a home in it, or about learning cross-country skiing, or planting the cherished garden in the springtime. Suddenly Sally began to look forward to escaping the nine-to-five work grind—not that I wanted to keep her from working, but after years of putting me through graduate school, Sally now looked forward to a long vacation. It was a happy time. I thought it was a time of renewed commitment between us. What an asshole.

The second week, our heat wave came to an end and we were getting restless out there anyway, so we hiked back to the car and took off for New Brunswick. There was another, less idyllic, week on an island off the coast where it rained all the time and our clothes started to smell. Finally, we headed back, cruising leisurely down the Atlantic shoreline toward Cambridge.

Back home, we junked most of our crummy Salvation Army furniture prefatory to the big move. It was that time of the year when Cambridge was at its worst—late August, no students or faculty around, the streets empty except for the winos, who clung to the steps of the Central Square post office like slugs on a garden wall. Our last night in town, we had dinner at the Blue Parrot. They were having a Hugo festival at the theater on Brattle Street, and Sally was dying to go, but I made her drive into Boston and see *Deliverance* instead.

You know how we felt that sweet August evening when we stood in the yard of our dream house on the Reddington campus. The months that followed lived up to our expectations for the Country Life.

Ever since that night at Bud Royce's house, after Mac's party, I suffered a growing, secret apprehension about how Sally would adapt to life in our new surroundings. I guess Bob Krock was right after all when he called me an "assumin' fellow." I certainly assumed for years that just getting Sally into the right bucolic setting would result, *bingo-bango*, in instant enduring happiness. What *was* I to assume? I didn't figure it was for nothing that she collected all those Country catalogs or daydreamed out loud on our scungy Cambridge sofa about the little house with the white picket fence—the house which was suddenly and amazingly and really *ours*.

Being of a bogus-psychoanalytical turn of mind back then, I tried to label Sally's Fourth of July freakout as "separation anxiety," you know, leaving tweedy old Cambridge, leaving her job, leaving her friends (Lisette and the golem), leaving all the familiar touchstones of life behind, blah, blah, blah. Otherwise, like any normal person, she needed friends. It was just unfortunate that she had to meet all the new candidates in the stiff, formal, and somewhat bizarre atmosphere of Mac's party. This, along with her tendency to make snap judgments, may have overloaded her circuits that night. In fact, though she could armor herself with a tough, icy veneer, Sally might have been even more nervous than I was. Basically we were just taking a big step in our lives, and I think she was simply frightened.

But when we arrived for good at the end of the summer, I was able to drop all these worries and morbid speculations. In that golden harvest time of the mutable Country year, Sally flung herself at her new life with all the verve of Leonard Bernstein conducting Vivaldi. The first couple of weeks, she worked indefatigable twenty-hour days getting the house shaped up, making curtains, painting rooms, stripping chairs and tables she cunningly gleaned from the antique stores which lined every lane in our part of the state. In September, she started a canning and pickling operation that would have put the Del Monte corporation to shame. Though we had no garden of our own that first fall, the roadside stands overflowed with produce, and my colleagues on the faculty, gardeners nearly all to a man (woman), couldn't give away enough of their zucchinis and tomatoes.

I bought cord upon cord of firewood, stacked the logs neatly in the yard, and finally learned to use a splitting maul after all those years of reading magazine articles about it. Before the weather even turned really cool, our house was filled, day and night, with the acrid perfume of woodsmoke. We burned cordwood the way Tibetans burn incense.

Then there was the cavalcade of paychecks as the first semester began. Remember, we didn't have to pay rent, so the money was mostly gravy. It was incredible after those years of penury. We went berserk buying appliances: a color TV, a huge stereo, Cuisinarts, coffee grinders, Toaster Ovens, Water Piks, shower-massagers, you name it, we bought it. It was grotesque in a way, I suppose, but also wonderful. After all those years of gazing longingly at the pages of the L.L. Bean catalog, we commenced filling out the order blanks with a vengeance. Each day, the postman's visit was Christmas. We took weekend jaunts to New York, stayed overnight in the

Biltmore, saw plays, caught Dylan and The Band at the Garden, ate in terrific restaurants. It was insane.

And also terrific. Was Sally happy? She sure seemed to be, or else she was doing a brilliant imitation of it. She looked great. She lost ten pounds. That morbid gray cast of the skin which afflicts all city dwellers turned to a rosy blush on her cheeks. Her eyes seemed as pale and pure as the blue mountain sky, her muscles grew stronger, her tummy got as hard as a washboard, and, in the course of things, thank God, she even found a friend.

By the middle of September, the Schusters and the Krocks were a kind of fearsome foursome. They were over at our place constantly, if not together, then separately. The arrangement agreed exactly with my idea of Country informality. On a mild September evening the four of us sat out on the front lawn with a pitcher of Piña Coladas, listening to the dry rustle of leaves in birch trees and the faraway notes of a guitar playing on some student's stereo in one of the dorms. I felt like the young lord of a peaceable kingdom, boundlessly serene.

One night, in October, we went to a drive-in movie in Bob's Chevy. It was a triple-feature horror show. We brought along a thermos jug of Margaritas, and at some point during the second feature the suggestion was made that we switch partners. I don't remember whose suggestion it was, though I don't believe it was mine. Sally and Annie switched seats. We were all pretty drunk, and it seemed perfectly innocent, even a little self-conscious. We all made big loud smooching noises and Bob and I took turns making panting sounds and it seemed like there was more laughter than anything else. Even so, I could not fail to notice the different smell of Annie's hair, the feel of her lips, the slightly salty taste of her skin. Inevitably, and in spite of all the clowning, the thought of what it would be like to sleep with her crossed my mind. I didn't have time to get truly paranoid, though, because at the same instant, and in the course of his smooching with my wife, Bob let out a resonant belch—as usual, he disdained cocktails for warm beer. Anyway, Sally called him "a pig" and bopped him over the head with a copy of the *Reddington Review* he had on the dashboard. A moment later Krock excused himself to take a wizz, and when he headed for the concession stand, I climbed out of the back and went around to take the driver's seat next to Sal. And that was pretty much the end of that night's experiment in retrograde teenage lust.

I guess we were all a little embarrassed by it, though. Two days later, a rainy afternoon, I came home from my last class and found Annie sitting at the kitchen table with a cup of coffee. Sally was nowhere in sight. There was an awkward moment, a quiet tremor of recognition between us that quickly metamorphosed into a little stab of anxiety in my stomach. Annie must have sensed it too. She was very fair-skinned, and when she blushed, her face got conspicuously red. She reached for her coffee, started to take a sip, but began giggling. I was afraid to even ask her what was so funny.

"I, uh . . . where's Sally?" I asked.

"Don't worry, you're safe," Annie said cryptically, only not cryptically enough for my peace of mind.

"I was just wondering," I said.

"Wondering what?"

"Where she was."

"Upstairs," Annie said, "in the bathroom."

"Then she's here."

"Yup."

"Well, that's what I was wondering."

Annie giggled some more and shook her head. To tell you the truth, the whole transaction was making me more and more nervous. Contrary to what Bob told me that night we drove around the campus, I did not yet feel like "a kid in a candy store," at least as far as the students were concerned. Not being a complete blockhead, I noticed the good-looking ones. At the student union snack bar, where I frequently stopped for a bite of lunch, my eyes would follow the path of a ripe little body poured into a leotard. But if my attention strayed now and again, it was only in the same sense that one might follow the lilting flight of a butterfly in the meadow, certainly without any attendant wish to gobble it up.

Also, aside from what Bob said that night at the Granary, I had no idea what his personal life with Annie was like, and I had a fierce desire to remain ignorant about it. Sometimes, the fantasies and fears that you bring to a situation get hopelessly mixed up with the observable facts, if there are such things as observable facts. Chesmire, the psychiatrist, would put it much better a year later: "Standard operating procedure is to go through life with your head up your ass," he would say, "in which case, what's to observe . . . ?"

Anyway, if I was attracted to Annie, then I didn't want to know about it, and if I couldn't help knowing about it, then I was determined not to dwell on it. Besides, Sally and I had an active sex life. Anybody else was out of the question.

So, what was the question?

I didn't want to find out.

Luckily, Sally came back down from the bathroom right after my weird little exchange with Annie, and the two of them drove off to buy some cider at the roadside stand. I poured myself a tumbler of chablis and sat down in the glow of the woodstove to read a stack of freshman comp themes.

Winter arrived one night in mid-November with a ten-inch snowfall, and the heavier snows that followed seemed to seal us off like volunteers in an Antarctic installation. Between midterm and final exams, and a blizzard of term papers, I found an excuse to hole up inside the house. Sally, on the other hand, bought a pair of cross-country skis, and took to the powdery hills and dales with the zeal of a Norwegian partisan patrolling for Nazis. We saw much less of the Krocks. Bob, mainly, came over a few Sunday afternoons in January for the football play-offs, but Annie, not a fan, did not come with him, and in a funny way, I was glad.

Around Valentine's Day, the faithful old Volvo threw a rod and died. For a few days I went into a kind of mourning and trudged through the knee-high snow to my classes in the rehabilitated village square a mile away. Then, one night I happened to be looking through our checkbook and realized there was almost 800 bucks in our account. The next day, Bob drove us down to the Datsun dealer on Route 7 where we plunked down $500 on a year-old station wagon. Our loan application to the Farmer's Exchange Bank of Reddington was approved before its three o'clock closing, and we drove the Datsun off the lot in time for supper. This was our initiation to the wonderful world of credit.

(The year before in Cambridge, as just another schmuck graduate student, I couldn't even get a measly $200 note to cover our bills. Now, suddenly, as a salaried pedagogue, my credit was top-drawer, first rate, four stars.)

Soon we were deluged with credit cards in the mail: Sears, Monkey Ward, Visa, Mobil Oil, the best of the gross national product ours for a flash of plastic. To top it off, within another month we had the engine of the old Volvo rebuilt, and like Lazarus it rose from the dead.

By April, Sally was deep in preparation for our Garden, that mythic centerpiece at the mushy heart of our Country dream. She laid out her strategy like General MacArthur planning his conquest of the Philippines. Our living room floor was covered with seedlings in split milk cartons. Planting and fertilization charts were pinned to the walls like campaign maps. Our brand-new gleaming gardening tools lay waiting in the hallway like weapons in an arsenal. Finally, the theoretical day of the last frost came and went and we hit the beach-heads of agriculture. I bought two little apple saplings at the local nursery. They were not expected to bear any fruit for four years, but in those days I was an optimist.

Then, one weekend in early May when you woke up in the morning to the singing of birds, and the hills and woods were ablaze with pale green fire, when spring seemed literally sprung on you overnight, one exquisite morning that could not have been more promising or perfect, Bob Krock decided to take me trout fishing.

Or rather, first he took me shopping, and then we went fishing.

He was very insistent about me buying the best equipment, so after my last class on a Friday we drove up to Orvis, the sportsmen's outfitters, in Manchester. There, I spent over $150 on a rod alone. Then, I had to have a reel, line, waders, a vest, a creel, flies, streamers, nymphs and microscopic "midges" with hooks so tiny a guppy might miss it. The metal box to keep your flies in (made in England!), had little compartments with spring-loaded windows and cost forty bucks by itself. I also had to have a trout knife, gadgets for disgorging hooks, for tying blood knots, for straightening leaders, for clipping tippets, not to mention bottles of dressings for sinking your fly, or floating your fly, or dressing your line or your leader. Krock was relentless.

"Look," he said, "if you want to be one of those assholes who just goes and kills fish, then get yourself a .357 magnum and go shoot carp in the Champlain canal. On the other hand, if you want to go *angling* with me and comport yourself like a sportsman and a gentleman then you just shut up and do like I tell you."

The salesman was happy to stay out of it, since Bob

was doing all his work for him. By the time we got out of there I was down over $300.

That evening Bob attempted to show me how to cast a fly line on the front lawn. We had a pitcher of daiquiris (and a six-pack of warm Miller's for Bob) and Annie and Sal were on hand to supply the wisecracks. I didn't dare tell Sal how much the junk really cost. By the time it was dark, I thought I just about had the knack of it.

I was wrong. The next day was one of the most frustrating days of my life. We drove up to the Battenkill, a legendary trout stream of the Northeast, to the stretch near the New York border. As soon as we got down into the stream, I realized it was one thing to cast a flyline on your lawn and quite another matter to do it where the fish are. First of all, the banks were overhung with branches. About half the time, my back-cast ended up in them and I lost half a dozen flies in the first twenty minutes. And when I managed to land one in the stream, it got snagged on branches hidden below the surface and I had to break off my leader. This was the real reason Ernest Hemingway blew his brains out, I thought.

Bob did not stick around and give me any more pointers either. He charged straight upstream and every time I tried to approach him he waved me back and shouted angrily. And he was catching fish too! Pulling them out of there left and right. Big bastards! I could have wrung his neck. I was so mad I wanted to smash my rod on the rocks and stomp on it. I didn't care how much it cost. But I was far too moderate a fellow back then—in all things, even my wrath—and I restrained myself.

Finally, around two in the afternoon Bob deigned to come back down and join me. I was sitting on a clay bank feeling sorry for myself. He said it was time for lunch.

"It's time to get the fuck away from here before I lose my marbles," I told him.

But he wouldn't hear of it. He said he wanted to fish

the afternoon rise, whatever that was. But first, he said, he wanted to fire up the fish in his creel for lunch.

So we tramped back to the car and took a portable grill out of the trunk of his rusty old Chevy and cooked the fish on his cruddy, rust-pocked hood.

"Why did you desert me like that?" I asked him. "I don't have the slightest idea how to go about this. You know I probably lost ten dollars worth of flies already this morning."

"Yeah," Bob said matter-of-factly with his mouth full of fish, "it's damned difficult, isn't it?"

"I thought you were going to teach me!"

"Heck, I taught you how to cast. You pretty much got to learn the rest yourself. Probably take you around two or three years before you get to where you can at least enjoy yourself and maybe catch somethin'."

"What . . . !"

"Well, maybe only one year, if you really apply yourself and practice a lot and read a few of the books."

"Why didn't you tell me that before?"

"I didn't want you to get discouraged."

"Oh, I see. How *do* you think I feel?"

"I dunno. You seem kind of discouraged, I guess."

"Yeah. Kind of."

"I suppose it's unavoidable."

"Jeeesh. . . ."

"Come on, man, eat your fish."

"I can't believe you tricked me into buying all this crap."

"I didn't trick you into anything," he said. He seemed to find the idea real funny and flecks of fish leaked out the corner of his mouth when he laughed. "Give it a chance. Stick with it, and one day you'll experience the profoundest joy."

"After three years, maybe?"

"You got to stick with it. It's like anything."

"I think I'll take up croquet instead."

"Go ahead. Be a damn sissy."

"Just watch me."

"I will. I'll set up a match for you with Mac. That's just the kind of damn fool recreation he'd love, croquet . . . . !"

"At least it's something you don't have to practice for three years."

"You'll get the hang of it, don't worry. Want a beer?"

"I want a hand grenade."

"That's not exactly sporting."

"I don't care."

"Want to smoke some?"

"I want to smoke lots."

"It's in the glove compartment."

I then commenced to get ripped out of my skull. My mood improved remarkably. I started noticing things. I was able to pay attention to something besides being pissed off.

After lunch Bob finally gave me permission to hang around with him and watch how he fished the afternoon rise. This "rise" turned out to be when the insect larvae swam to the surface of the stream, shed their skins, and flew off as adult mayflies. It drove the trout crazy, Bob said, and I could see fish rising to the surface and dimpling the water as they gulped bugs out of the film. Bob's casting was impeccable. He laid his line out in perfect loops and his flies dropped to the water like little paratroopers.

He must have hooked over a dozen fish inside of the hour or so the rise lasted. He released all but a few back into the stream. I didn't catch anything, naturally. On the way back to the car, though, I asked him to lend me a couple of fish so Sally wouldn't think I was a feeb. When we got back to Reddington, we learned that Peggy Royce was in the hospital.

*   *   *

The precipitating event was that Bud came home and caught her trying to insert the blade of a screwdriver into an electrical outlet. It was only the most glaring facet of a longstanding and systematic suicide attempt. We all knew that she was a heavy user—abuser—of barbiturates. But up to that point we also all pitched in to help Bud maintain the polite fiction of Peggy's poor health, her "illness," as if she was the victim of some vague, genteel disease like simple anemia. This glossing-over was our fucked up way of respecting the Royce's privacy.

What we didn't know just then was that for about ten days before the incident, Peggy had stopped taking care of herself entirely, stopped eating, soiled the bed she refused to leave. By the time Bud brought her into Reddington's small general hospital, she weighed less than eighty pounds. She was admitted directly to the psychiatric unit.

Because she was so physically fragile, the doctor decided to maintain her dosage of Seconal for a while, pump some nutrients into her, and then slowly wean Peggy off the barbiturate. Simple withdrawal, he said, would kill her. At the time of her admission, though, Peggy herself would not communicate. There was some question of organic brain damage from her years of prior usage. She foiled the staff's plan from the outset by continuing to refuse nourishment. Her legs began to curl underneath in a sort of fetal position, and she developed sores where her pelvic bones rested against the mattress.

The therapist assigned to her was a nerveless young Nazi of a clinical psychologist who held the view that Peggy's behavior comprised a sort of lethal "game." She was "on strike" in effect, he explained to Bud in Peggy's unresponsive presence, and added that if she kept it up, she was liable to die. The therapist's policy was to be "up front" with his patients and the members of their families. It was neither "ethical" nor "useful" to discuss patients' problems behind their backs, he said. A given patient's "craziness" was more than likely only a "symptom" of a crazy relationship, he explained. So, the three of them sat together day after day trying to hash out the particulars of Peggy and Bud's marriage. It might have been good theory, but it wasn't much help. There's no doubt that Bud was half in the bag during those sessions. I know because Bob Krock and I took turns driving him to the hospital and I could smell the whiskey on his breath.

During the second week, the Royce's son from Princeton came up, and together he, Bud and the therapist plumbed the family's history while Peggy stared into the ceiling. In his nerveless voice, the therapist repeated his prognosis, as if it was the next best thing to a bucket of cold water in the face. In his anguish and helplessness, Bud broke down, screamed at her to not die, and had to be assisted from the room.

The staff next debated whether to start I.V.'s on her or send her up to Intensive Care and have them do it. The therapist thought it was wrong to "help her play her death game," but the doctors must have outvoted him. They transferred her upstairs and started the I.V.'s. As soon as the tubes were inserted and taped in place, Peggy tore them out. She was put on "constant observation" with a nurse stationed at her bedside and vital signs taken every fifteen minutes. Soon, feeble but unrelenting, she caught a cold. In half a day, it became simple pneumonia. Two days later, Peggy died.

"I killed her. I killed her with my drinking," Bud repeated to himself through the entire funeral, from the service to the graveside at the cemetery in North Adams, where he buried her next to her father and mother. "I killed her with my drinking."

We all told him it wasn't true, but I'm not sure how many of us secretly agreed—only with some important reservations. We knew a few of the reasons for Bud's drinking, and one in particular was present at the funeral service. Afterward, Mac took Bud aside and spoke to him for several minutes, the younger man's hand on Bud's shoulder in a strange, fatherly way, and Bud nodding his head slightly. None of us overheard the conversation or ever learned what it was about.

Soon, the same helplessness we all felt about Peggy suddenly shifted to Bud. His drinking became continuous and suicidal. It was around finals time and Bob Krock made up the exams for Bud's courses, with the rest of us pitching in to grade them. Meanwhile, Bud was turning into a basket-case. We took turns spending time with him, first in the evenings and for dinner, then round-the-clock. We were afraid to leave him alone. He had already driven his car through the garage door. The sons were no help either. The one from Princeton blamed Bud for his mother's death and went home to New Jersey right after the funeral. The younger one was a little too fond of drinking himself, and *we* urged him to go back to Boulder. Something had to be done.

It was suggested that Bud find a safe place to get off the sauce. Reddington Hospital was out of the question, after the experience with Peggy. Bob and Annie looked around and settled on the Institute for Living, an expensive clinic in Connecticut. They drove him down the next day.

He did get off the booze. It took some doing, but he beat his addiction and started getting a grip back on himself and his life. We visited him at the end of August and he seemed to really be getting his act together. I could see now what Bob meant when he had alluded to "the Bud Royce who brought me to Reddington." He went through a complete personality change when he wasn't drinking. And now he was even beginning to make plans for the future—the healthiest sign. He wanted to take a sabbatical in the fall and visit Greece. He laughed when Bob told him about our fishing hijinks.

Driving back to Vermont that night we were full of

optimism that he was going to make it after all. The next day there was a phone call from Hartford. Bud had a heart attack during the night and died quietly in his sleep.

Guess who got his job?

It was about the time of Bud Royce's death that I undertook to start my first novel: *Honniker's Progress*. The main character, you see, was a fellow named Honniker, and the idea was to show him making his way in the world. Sound kind of vague? Well, it was my first novel and there was a certain amount of, shall we say, floundering at the beginning. Anyway, by the time the fall term started, I had done one chapter. Sally, always so generous in her praise, liked to refer to my book as *Honker's Regress*. She had a point, but she could have kept it to herself.

six

Sally Schuster, née Sally Parsifal. Dear one. Does she seem shadowy to you? Now you will hear all about this obdurate creature, my dream girl. I choose this opportunity because, as you will see, the condition of our marriage began to deteriorate sharply around the start of our second year at Reddington, and I wouldn't want you to get a distorted idea that it was always like that. For all her character deformities, I loved her.

When I think of the times before, first in Washington where we met and wed, then New York, Cambridge and finally Reddington, I see that I was largely unconscious through the whole long transit. Our lives followed the prescribed pattern for young gringo marrieds—an oblivious passage toward dimly realized or unagreed-upon goals. Aside from our apparent mutual desire to escape city life for The Country, I wonder now if there were any other intersections between us. So, it's probably no surprise that when we finally did arrive in The Country, our lives started to veer drastically.

Since I was only married to her and did not inhabit

her brain or body, I will describe the significant events of
her history and behavior as they were known to me. If
these details shed insufficient light on her true nature, or
fail to uncover those hidden wellsprings which animated
her, which directed her mysterious movements, then you
will know as much as I do, or neither of us will ever
know.

Her grandfather was a federal judge of a district
which, at that time, included Maryland, Delaware and
part of Pennsylvania. He had connections with the
powerful Tydings family and so contrived to have his
eldest son, Robert Parsifal, elected to a congressional seat
in the Washington, D.C. suburbs, right across the Maryland line. This was Sally's father.

Robert Parsifal married Mary Meigs, daughter of the
late Republican representative from the 17th district of
Ohio. This was Sally's mother. The couple, Robert and
Mary, had three children whom they named Elizabeth,
Macy and Robert, Jr. What? No Sally? That's right. At
least not until seventeen years after Bob, Jr. What a
surprise!

Or a mistake.

She came into this world when her mother and father
were forty-four and fifty-five respectively. This alone may
suggest unhappy beginnings. She was a difficult birth.
(Sally once told me that the first three months of her
pregnancy, her mother thought she had a duodenal ulcer,
so far from the forefront of her mind was the very idea of
motherhood at that late date. And it was only the yet
more horrifying suspicion of uterine cancer which drove
her to the doctor's office where she soon got the incredible news that it was just another little one on the way.)

She barely knew her brothers and sisters. They were
more like aunts and uncles. Brother Bob, Jr. was on his
way to Dartmouth the very day she was born. Sister Macy

had been cutting capers at Wellesley for three years already. And sister Liz was married to one of Harlan F. Stone's law clerks and was a mother herself!

Her parents were not deliberately cruel or indifferent. They just didn't know what to do with her. By the time Sally was a speaking, running and reasonable child, her parents were practically old fogies. What did they know about raising a child in the age of TV, Sputnik and Hula-Hoops? Lord knows it had been hard enough during the era of Shirley Temple, the Green Hornet and Adolf Hitler. Besides, how could they help but think of her as some kind of a freak?

Never very ambitious, Sally's father clung to his safe congressional seat through war, depression, recovery, war, cold war and New Frontier. He had no higher aspirations. He liked Congress. It was the best country club in America. And it gave its members just enough work to take their minds off of drinking and golf.

With the other children grown up and long gone, Sally rattled around the thirty-room house on the Bethesda estate like a BB in a packing crate. Her daily activities were supervised by a succession of nurses, nannies and maids. She saw her parents each night at supper. It was a sort of togetherness, I suppose. (Remember, the space between particles in an atom corresponds roughly to the space between planets in our solar system.) At age twelve, Sally was shipped off to prep school.

She always said that she "didn't mind" being sent away to school, and the casual observer might nod understandingly. But what's less obvious is how this comprised a comprehensive attitude about life in general, and especially personal calamities. Like the time she told me that she "didn't mind" getting an abortion. It was an uncanny attitude of indifference in the face of pain.

Anyway, she spent the next six years of her life at the Foxhall School in Edneyville, Virginia, where she suffered the usual sorrows and depredations endemic to that mode of education (loneliness, petty jealousies, the brutality of strangers), and where she also learned to enjoy some of life's more rudimentary gratifications. Perhaps *enjoy* is not exactly the right word.

No, my sweet Sally was not a virgin when I married her. Who is these days? She lost her cherry at age fifteen to a VMI cadet named Darvel Daniel Dunsten from Charleston, South Carolina. Wherever you are today, Dar, whatever theater of war you're preparing yourself for, whatever missile silo or ship-of-the-line you are in charge of, please know that there are no hard feelings. I would have done the same thing to your future wife, or your sister.

Did he have to ply her with liquor and drugs to pluck that little fruit? No. She saw him at one of the deb balls so popular with youngsters of her ethnic persuasion. There he was: ramrod straight in his formal white tunic, and so touchingly out of place in his crew-cut next to the leering, long-haired Andover boys in their brothers' hand-me-down dinner jackets, and their eyes bloodshot with wacky weed. Anyway, there was dumb-looking Dar in his uniform. She went after *him*, got *him* drunk, dragged him outside beyond the portico, unfastened his numerous belts and sashes, and told him to "take it."

When he said, "take what . . . ?" she had to spell it out for him.

And that's where it happened: twenty feet from the west parking lot of Baltimore's Bridgestone Country Club. She dated him for a couple of weekends, then ditched him for a Rehoboth Beach lifeguard. After him, why it was simply more boys than you could shake a stick at. She lost count.

At eighteen, she entered plain old middlebrow George Washington University in Washington, D.C. for the simple reason that a dude she had suddenly grown serious about was a student at nearby Georgetown Law. No, not me. I'm talking about Franklin P. Osborne, presently an assistant to the United States Attorney for the state of Rhode Island—but back then, just a Wisconsin Avenue lounge lizard with a pedigree as long as the Lincoln Memorial reflecting pool.

Sally says that Frank broke her heart when he dumped her. This is a prime example of the sort of confusion Sally was prone to. After all, I had entered the scene long before the curtain dropped on that romance. Sally just liked to use it against me when she thought I was behaving poorly. Just as she seemed to enjoy referring to me as "a jew bastard." This, of course, was prior to her career in social work. In her prime, Sally was a regular yahoo. Actually, I think it was Frank who started the whole "jew bastard" thing, but Sally must have liked the ring of it. It made me something of an exotic in her eyes. I don't think she cared much about defying the epochal tide of Aryan culture.

What was it about her that I liked so much? Well, for one thing, in case you haven't gathered it already, Sally was a knockout. She was tall, about five six in flat shoes and athletically lanky. Her hair was the most marvelous ash-blonde color and she had two streaks of white which grew out of either side of the part, and which she swept back. She had had the streaks ever since she was a little girl. Her eyes were pale blue-gray, like a rainy sky. Her nose, oddly enough, was not the pert little standard of gringo beauty. It was just a bit flat and somewhat broad at the bridge, but it was a very pretty nose.

Her mouth was full of surprising nuances of expression. In repose her lips didn't quite cover the tips of her upper front teeth. This gave her just a slightly buck-toothed look, as if she was on the verge of asking you a question. When she smiled, the lip rolled upward to reveal orthodontically perfect choppers. She wore virtually no make-up and looked better without it than any woman I've ever known.

So much for the front of her head. Proceeding downward, the next salient feature was that constellation of freckles over her collarbone and spreading into the hollow between her breasts. They were the result of a decade of Rehoboth Beach sunshine. I remember trying to lick them off during those first febrile sessions with her in my apartment on 20th Street, when Frank Osborne was supposedly ditching her and breaking her heart and she sought comfort in my "jew bastard" arms.

Her breasts—Iiiyyy! God! After all the unpleasantries of the year gone by I quail before the memory of them still. They were monuments beside which the clean round classical lines of, say, the Capitol dome evoked a mere potato in comparison. They were as round and firm as Spanish melons and stood out proudly, arrogantly, as if daring to be seized and devoured. Holding them up were firm slabs of pectoral muscle which tucked into flawless, milk-white underarms. (A hygiene nut, Sally continued to shave there even at the height of the Feminist hysteria— circa 1970–1973.)

The aureoles at the leading edge of each perfect breast were a pink color such as is found only on the insides of certain rare, tropical seashells from the Great Barrier Reef. The nipples were perfect pink buttons. These glands were simply magnificent. I used to like to lie with my head in her lap while she sat up in bed, and stare at their sweeping, parabolic undersides. For what turned out to be her manifold incertitudes about sex generally, Sally sure loved to show her breasts off.

When bralessness became the rage, oh, about 1968 I'd say, Sally junked hers with the verve of a twenty-dollar hooker. Those fabulous glands of hers commanded the attention of all as she (they) sashayed now to the left, now to the right, on her way to a sociology class of a sweet, cherryblossom morning by the Potomac. Frequently she disrupted traffic along 21st Street, G.W.U.'s main drag. She even took to wearing semi-see-thru outfits on public occasions (at the wedding reception of a niece, for example—sister Liz's kid, eight months *older* than Sal—she showed up in a little shift the exact weight and texture of Kleenex and stole the show). What a vixen! I could feasibly discourse endlessly on the subject of her breasts, but by now I'm sure you get the picture: great tits.

Moving right along then, she was long-waisted and her belly was a sleek oval like the rounded underside of a fine porcelain platter. Her hips were perhaps a little narrow for some tastes, but to me they were perfect, and made less severe by those trim, flabless buttocks the precise color of peach ice cream within the permanent tattoo of a bikini bottom.

Finally, we arrive at that shrine-like organ between her legs. In some women this area is a forbidding odoriferous maw of coarse hair and scary pink flaps. Sally's pussy was more like a bonbon filled with raspberry cream. Other times, it seemed a slippery orchid, each tender pink fold a marvel of symmetry and the clitoris a shy button beneath its pink cowl of flesh. It gave off the subtlest of fragrances and flavors—not the swamp-stink of some. It could be a daffodil, lightly salted butter, lobster bisque (a hint of sherry in the sauce), cherry jam. I nuzzled it for hours staring upward between her long deer-like legs. When I attempted to share my thoughts with her on the subject of her pussy, Sally said, "how nice."

Let's face it: there are parts of her, physical parts, which seem in my own mind to have a separate existence from her character, her person-hood, and which I will never be able to traduce or profane. Physically, she was a wonder. I'll never meet one like her again. Maybe I am even more of a baboon than I am willing to admit.

Did I neglect to mention her arms, her hands, the lobes of her ears, her feet, her ankles, those twin dimples above her dairy-fresh derrière. Just thinking about that body again leaves me limp, feeble, giddy with a weird kind of retrograde desire. Also wonder and nausea.

She gave the best blow-jobs the world has ever known, none of your hurry-up, pucker-and-run affairs, but long, lingering, devastating hours of maniacal artistry. Out of a single woodwind she evoked whole symphonies. She was not half bad with a mere hand, either, committing outrages in unlikely places: beaches, cars, theaters, offices, for example, and once under the table in a crowded Howard Johnson's off the Pennsylvania Turnpike.

In bed of more than a thousand nights she was peerless, knees thrown back and her entire, pink, wet bottom open to me as though it would be hardly a trick for her to turn entirely inside out, as only mollusks can do. Or waking me in the morning by sweeping those silky pillows of bosom over my trunk and hips, then climbing aboard, clinging and rocking in our waterbed like dolphins mating in the shifting tides of some equatorial sea, so lovely and liquid and warm. And Franklin Plumrose Osborne was breaking her heart? In a pig's ear! She was mine, Franklin, you uptight Wasp prosecuting asshole attorney with your fucking pedigree and your family's ticket stubs from the fucking Mayflower! Fuck you!

I am losing my head.

We were married at the end of my senior year, her junior, at G.W.U. The ceremony was held on a gorgeous day at her parents' estate in Bethesda under the magnolia trees on the lawn. (The old couple is very much alive to this day, ages eighty-five and seventy-four. Last time I saw him, though, "Dad" was beginning to show signs of incipient senility. He kept calling me "Bob".) The wedding was nonsectarian, since Sally's folks were only nominal Congregationalists and my own parents indifferent Hebrews. It was conducted by Liz's husband, now a judge of the Maryland Court of Appeals. A host of minor celebrities was present: several congressmen, a well-known Washington columnist, a retired baseball commissioner, a cabinet officer and a handful of socialites.

We honeymooned in Puerto Rico. Sally caught a 250-pound hammerhead shark from a charter boat. We drank a lot of Piña Coladas and strolled hand in hand down the long, deserted beaches of Cabo Rojo, pausing now and then to make love in a cove, a grotto, under a coconut tree. I believed I was the luckiest guy in the world. Belief, Chesmire used to say, is 99 percent of our reality. The remaining 1 percent, he said, is truth. Poor guy, he was right.

From this point on you already know most of the details. When I started grad school at Columbia the following fall, Sally finished her BA at Barnard. Then she got her job with the parole board. We were on our way in the land of opportunity.

What was it that upset our little apple cart? Reddington? No, not exactly. I'm not even convinced it was the fulfillment of our Country Life fantasy, though I'm sure that was part of it. It had more to do with the end of that peculiar state of semiconsciousness which dogged me through the multiple stages of our marriage. It was like coming out of a dense fog after traveling thousands of miles for years and years, just automatically putting one foot in front of the other, oblivious to the shrouded but changing landscape. It was partly a matter of being there, yet not really being there. Obviously, I was not in a complete coma, else how would I have tied my shoes, let alone gotten those degrees and a teaching job, let alone remembered any of it? No, this was a slyer, more subtle form of brain damage—the kind that proceeds from dishonesty. The kind that distorts the truth of things to the degree that one is no longer living a life so much as a wishful simulation of it.

It was the night before the first day of classes of my second fall semester. Bud Royce had been dead for a month and we were resuming normal life. Mac MacWhorter had been appointed Acting Chairman of the department while a search committee commenced its task of seeking a permanent Chairman. (Mac was also Chairman of the search committee, and who didn't wonder how he would contrive to root himself out of the thickets as the logical candidate.) Otherwise, he was on his best behavior.

We were having an ordinary, peaceful, lazy, Sunday night at home. It was chilly and we had a fire going. The house was full of the smell of woodsmoke. We had the classical music station from Albany on the stereo. They were playing something quietly histrionic, some Beethoven piano thing. After dinner, Sally went to work repotting some plants while I headed upstairs to the spare bedroom I used as an office to work on *Honniker's Progress*. For some reason, Sally was in a provocative mood. Only the way she expressed it was to pretend to be amused. Anyway, she stopped me on the stairway to ask how come she never heard much typing up there.

"Writing a novel isn't just pecking at a typewriter," I explained to her. "You have to think a lot. Plan things. Then you type."

"You speak from experience, I take it," she said.

"I'm doing it, aren't I?"

"Sure," she hastened to agree. "What's going to happen tonight?"

"Happen?"

"In the novel."

"I'm not really sure yet. That's part of the mystery of the creative experience. It just sort of springs full-blown onto the page, if you know what I mean."

"Not really," she said. "I mean, you just said that you have to plan things and think a lot, so obviously it doesn't spring full-blown."

"Well, sometimes it does. And sometimes it doesn't."

"I see," she said. "So, where did you get the idea for this Honker of yours to grow up on an avocado plantation?"

"It may please you to know that it's no longer an avocado plantation."

"No? You changed it?"

"Yes. It's a mink ranch."

"Oh, that's great."

"You think so?"

"For sure. Is he still depressed all the time, this Honker?"

"He has an unhappy childhood."

"Who wouldn't? On a mink ranch."

"I don't know, Sal. I don't know anybody who ever grew up on one."

"So why the heck are you writing about one?"

"It's fiction, darling. I make it up as I go along. It's not autobiography. And if you're such a stickler for fast-paced action drama, then how come you dragged me off to all those fucking Hugo movies. Talk about *boring!*"

"They were sensitive films. And they weren't all the same either. You have no powers of discernment."

"I don't, huh?"

"None whatsoever—as far as foreign films go."

I started to reply but suddenly realized how upset I was getting and didn't want to ruin the chance of getting

some work done by escalating the ridiculous argument.
But Sally was relentless.

Why don't you write about something you *do* know
about   she said.

I climbed halfway up the stairs, then stopped and
turned back.

'Why don't you get off my case, Sally?"

She threw up her hands.

"See," she said, "you can't even take a little criticism.
That's a real sign of insecurity in your art. I give you my
honest reaction and what happens? You freak out."

'I am not freaking out. Do I look like I'm freaking
out? Am I swinging from the chandelier? Am I smashing
crockery? No. Clearly I am on my way upstairs to apply
the seat of my pants to the seat of a chair. To work. And
as for criticism, I think you ought to know that there is a
difference between criticism and mockery. I, for one,
discern that there is a difference."

'I m not mocking you."

'What do you call it then? Encouragement?"

'It's just being honest. Just because we're married
doesn t mean I can't be honest."

'Then how come you keep calling him Honker, huh?
His name is Honniker, not Honker, and you know it."

I m being playful."

Oh, really? I thought it was mockery."

I wasn't mocking."

See you later, Sally."

I continued up the stairway to the office and closed
the door emphatically. But I did find it difficult to get
started For all her sarcasm there was a grain of truth to
what Sally was saying, at least about the plot of my novel.
There wasn't much in the way of real action. So far all
Honniker was doing was being depressed and unhappy.
And moping around the old mink ranch. I had nineteen-
and-a half pages of manuscript. At least I had gotten him

through his childhood economically. But there was just something terribly wrong with the whole beginning. I racked my brain for more than an hour trying to figure out where I went wrong. Meanwhile, I smoked about twenty cigarettes, and when I wasn't doing that, I was carving down pencils with my hunting knife until they were just little metal capsules with an eraser at one end. Finally, though, I realized what was wrong with the mink ranch. It wasn't depressing *enough*! I had to set the action of his boyhood in a place that would really *justify* his being depressed all the time.

So I changed the scene to the steel mills in Pittsburgh. His mother is this society girl who marries beneath herself to this big, beefy German immigrant steelworker. Her father, a rich banker, disowns her. After the first few years of marriage, the glow of bestial love wears off. She starts to loathe the grim drudgery of the blue-collar life. She grows so bitter that she begins to hate and resent everything, even her little son, Peter (Honniker). Then, her husband, Max, is killed in this accident at the mill, so Honniker has to go out to work at the age of twelve to support his mother. It's 1934. The whole country is in a huge depression, including Honniker. I liked that.

By midnight, I had the whole first chapter rewritten. I tidied up my desk and swept all the pencil shavings into the wastebasket. Then, humming "I Am The Walrus," I tiptoed next door to our bedroom. Sally was sitting up in bed reading. She was wearing her reading glasses and looked up at me over the rims.

"Sounded like you were going great guns," she said.

"Yeah, I revised the whole first chapter."

"You get him off that mink ranch?"

"Oh, yes. It's a steel mill now," I told her proudly. Then I related the whole new story. She seemed to be listening patiently, but when I was done, she stared at me as if I had told a joke and she missed the punchline, or expected more. "It's just the beginning," I tried to explain.

"But he's still depressed all the time."

"Of course he is. His life is hell. His family, his mother, the whole thing. This is what makes him so bitter in the long run. This is how I get to turn him into a real meanie later on."

Sally took off her glasses, closed her book and put them both on the night-table.

"There are two things I don't get about this story of yours. In the first place, how come the main character turns out to be a bad guy?"

"He's *not* a bad guy in the ordinary sense. He's just a guy who gets twisted by his environment. That's what it's all about. How he gets turned into a bastard by these immutable forces."

"But how are we supposed to identify with him if he's such a bastard?"

"Identify?"

"Yeah. I mean, why should we care about him if he's such a bastard and depressed all the time and doesn't have any good qualities?"

"That's the whole point. It's a tragedy. You're supposed to sympathize with him for turning into such a bastard. You sympathize with Shylock, don't you?"

"Yeah, but he's got a kind of integrity. And guts. Those are good qualities," Sally said. "What's your Honker got?"

"He—I wish you'd cut that out!"

"What?"

"Calling him Honker."

"Sorry."

"No, really."

"I said I'm sorry. I swear I'll quit it. But tell me: what's he got in the way of good qualities?"

"He . . . works hard."

"So did Adolf Hitler."

"He, uh, perseveres in the face of hardship."

"Ditto."

"Aw, for Chrissake, Sally. Give me a chance to work it out, will you? It's only the first chapter."

"Okay, okay. But you see what I mean, don't you? About being able to identify?"

"Jesus! Who's the English teacher around here, huh?"

"Okay," Sally said. "Forget it."

"No. Wait a minute. Let's not just forget it. I mean, who are you, anyway? A retired paper-shuffler? A former bureaucrat! I spent the last ten years of my life busting my hump to get credentials and now you're gonna lecture me about literature!"

"I'm a paper-shuffler, huh? That takes away my right to hold an opinion?"

"You've got your right. Nobody's taking away your right."

"*You* are. You're disqualifying me because I don't have some stupid degree. I read more goddam books in a week than you read in six months."

"You do not!"

"I do too! Name all the books you read this week," Sally said.

That really pissed me off. We belonged to about three book clubs. Sally had a whole pile of hardcover best sellers on her night-table. I felt trapped.

"Don't pull that kind of shit on me," I said. "I have to work for a living. You can read all the livelong day if you like. Me? I have to go to work."

"Ha! You call that work? Teaching two classes three days a week. You have four goddamn days off!"

"That's just in the summer, Sally. You know that."

"Well, come on! You said you were so busy working for a living you can't stop and read a book. And it's obviously not true."

"Okay, you win. You read more than me. I'm a phoney. I'm a fraud. I'm a nothing—"

"I didn't say that—"

"All I do is spend six hours a night trying to write a novel. What a lame excuse for a human being—"

"Maybe for a novel. Not for a hu—"

"Ah-ha! So, you think my novel's lame? The raw truth finally comes out—"

"And you don't spend six hours a night on it, either. This is the first time in a week, as a matter of fact, if I'm not mistaken. Come on Rich, you've written the first chapter over four times now."

"You think it's easy? You think you just sit down and the whole thing comes out full-blown, or something. I've got news for you: literature is not made that way—"

"Really . . . ?"

"Yes, really. Did you ever try to do it? Why don't you give it a try sometime and tell me how easy it is?"

"Maybe I will."

"Fine. Go ahead."

I wasn't even angry anymore. Just tired and demoralized and burned out. I took off my clothes, crawled into bed with my back to Sally, and turned out the light on my night-table. But it was impossible to fall asleep. I must have lain there for half an hour running the whole idiotic, demoralizing conversation through my head. The more I thought about it, the more I felt like an asshole, but also partly the victim of injustice. Finally, I rolled over and snuggled next to Sally, who had resumed her reading.

"Why are you picking on me like this?" I asked her.

"Who's picking on anybody?"

Clearly, this was not the right approach to take with Sally, the champion denial artist of the world.

"Why are we having this argument?" I rephrased it.

"I don't know," she said, sounding sincerely puzzled.

"It seems to me that you started it." Whoops. Another tactical blunder.

"I don't see how you can possibly blame me," she said.

"Okay, you're right. It takes two to tango."

"It sure does."

"I mean, it's a two-way street."

"It sure is."

"Hon, take off your glasses and let's make love."

Sally looked down at me and sighed.

"Not now, Rich."

"Come on, Sal. It'll help us make up."

"I . . . I don't feel like it right now, Rich."

"What: making up or making love?"

"Love."

"Oh. You don't?"

She shook her head.

"What is it? You get your period or something?" I slipped my hand between her legs.

"Cut that out, will ya!" she said and removed my hand forcibly. "I told you, I just don't feel like it. Now, go to sleep."

"There's got to be some reason."

"I told you already. I just don't feel like it."

"That's not a reason. Tell me *how come* you don't feel like it."

"I just don't, that's all. Now, will you bug off. And quit sticking your hand in there!"

"What's wrong with you tonight?"

"Nothing."

Poor question. Why would I think there might be something the matter? What would put such an idea into my head? I squelched an impulse to throttle her, right there in bed. It would've been a real novelty in our relationship, which up until then had not included punching. But instead of socking her one, I did something which our relationship *had* included before: I raped her

I removed her glasses and chucked them aside on the carpet I think she realized something funny was up, because her upper lip curled into a sort of sneer. But before there could be any further discussion, I threw her book across the room, pinned her to the mattress, threw up the skirts of her nightgown, climbed aboard, and humped her like a German shepherd, complete with grunts barks and howls. She resisted slightly at first, and then realizing it was no use, gave in. Soon, she was panting and moaning. We came at the same moment, and rather quickly, you might say. I clung to her briefly in the exhausted aftermath, then rolled off and lit a cigarette.

Feeling better now?" I inquired.

Must you always smoke afterward?"

I always do," I replied a little defensively, in a voice that sounded too whiny for my own tastes. "You know that I always do. And you haven't answered my question

What question?"

How do you feel now?"

Oh, I see, I'm supposed to feel better now, is that it? After you jump me like a bull moose? After you assault me? Well, the answer is, I feel . . . violated."

Come on. You love it when I do that."

Dream on, buster."

'You used to. You used to ask me for it."

For that? I can't imagine what possessed me. I asked to be . . *reamed*? No, I don't think I ever requested it quite that way."

Maybe not in those words. But you used to enjoy it.

"I never enjoyed it that way. It's boorish if you want my opinion."

"How come you never said so before?"

"I don't know. Can't we just go to sleep now?"

She pulled down her nightgown, which was all askew, and fluffed up her pillow.

"Just a second here," I said. "You can't just drop a hot potato like that in my lap and then nod off."

"I'm tired, Rich."

"I want to know why you never said so before."

"Said what?"

"That you didn't like it."

"Like what?"

"Oh cut it out. You know what—"

"I just don't want to discuss it."

"Well, that's obvious. Are you saying you *never* enjoyed it? Not once?"

Sally started making these loud snoring noises, like kids make when they're playacting "sleep."

"Sally, I'm not fooling around anymore. I want you to explain what you said."

"Oh what, for Godsake?"

"You *never* enjoyed it?"

"No."

"Not once?"

"No. Never, ever, not once."

"Jeez . . ."

I couldn't believe what was happening. Anger, fear, despair, rage, sadness, all whirled in hellish combinations and finally melded into a kind of shock which is the brain's way of stalling for time.

"What about just now?" I asked her in a trembling voice.

"What about it?" she mumbled into her pillow.

"You didn't enjoy that?"

"Not in the least."

"Then what were all those noises you were making?"

"Encouragement. So you would hurry up and get it over with."

"Aw, you gotta be kidding me . . ."

"No. Honest Injun."

"Aw, Sally . . ."

"Isn't that what you asked for downstairs? Encouragement?"

"This is really diabolical . . ."

"No, it's what you asked for."

"It is *not*! And you know it!" I realized I better lower my voice. "Tell me something: does all this apply to when you came?"

"When I came . . . ?"

"Yes, *came*, goddammit, as in orgasm, as in got your rocks off!"

"I never came."

"You didn't?"

"I faked it."

The next sound that was heard in this dimly lighted room cannot be precisely reproduced here. Imagine a forlorn prairie landscape at that hour which is neither night nor day. There is an endless purple horizon. The cry of a large animal can be heard way off in the distance. The beast cannot be seen, but you know that it has been badly wounded.

I have a theory about honesty. ("Mr. Theory," Sally used to call me.) Anyway, this is it: in order to be truly honest with other people, you must be 100 percent honest with them at all times. This might sound impossible, but I don't think so. Permit me to explain the reasoning behind it.

Let's say my friend Joe tells me he's found this great way to rip off the supermarket. He justifies this thievery, i.e., dishonesty, by saying that he's really broke and hungry, and besides, the supermarket is just ripping off the little guy (himself) all the time anyway, so he's just getting even.

Fine, I reply, but what if I had something he really needed and was too broke to buy and what if I wasn't willing to part with it. Would he rip me off for it, then?

No, Joe says, I'm his friend. He wouldn't rip me off.

But what if he was really desperate? The point is, how do I know when he is or isn't desperate enough to deal with *me* dishonestly, to use his desperation as a way to justify ripping me off? The fact is, I don't know. If he's willing to be dishonest over a trivial matter, like stealing a pack of Hostess Twinkies from the supermarket, then how would he act when something really important is at stake?

No, the truth is, I'll never be able to trust him again. When you find that a person is not being 100 percent honest with you, you've got a serious situation on your hands, my friends.

Imagine how I felt, then, when Sally said she faked her orgasm to "encourage" me to hurry up and finish. Naturally, I could hardly sleep for the rest of the night. Nor did my condition improve by the dawn's early light. It only got worse. My anxiety seemed to grow exponentially as the day wore on, and by my third class of that brand-new semester I was coiled behind my desk in spasms of nausea and apprehension, and dismissed the group after telling them what textbooks they needed for the course.

See, the thing that tormented me was the idea that if Sally was willing to fake an orgasm in one situation, what would prevent her from faking it in other situations—or every situation! The implications, as you can see, were kind of spooky. And the worst part of all was just not knowing. So, I decided to put the question to her that night.

I was going to ask her during dinner, but I just couldn't come out with it, and sat there glumly stuffing my face with Sally's chicken with snow peas and rice. Then, we watched one stupid TV show after another and I must have chickened out fifty times. Finally, when we went upstairs to bed, I was able to marshal my courage and put it to her. She was flitting around the room in her nightgown, patting lotions on her cheeks, eye sockets, forehead; plucking little hairs here and there, taking out her contact lenses. I was watching her the whole time from the bed, following her progress around the room, as if she was an unusually large and dangerous moth.

"How long have you been faking orgasms?" I asked her.

"Is that what's been bugging you tonight?"

"Yes."

"I thought something was bugging you."

"Now that we've established that something's been bugging me, how's about answering the question?"

"And what was the question again?"

"Faking," I reminded her emphatically. "If you think you're going to weasel your way out, forget it."

"Who's weaseling?"

"Answer the question!"

"You want to know why I faked it?"

"No. That's not what I asked you. I want to know how long, how many times, in how many instances. And I want a fucking answer from you, not a bunch of distracting questions!"

There was a pause as Sally set down a plastic jar of lotion on her dressing table.

"Now and then," she finally said, "if you must know."

"Can you narrow that down. Does 'now and then' mean every other time, or just on Groundhog Day, or what? What does it mean?"

"God, Rich, you want dates?"

"No! Not dates! I don't want to know dates, goddammit! I want to know the frequency that you fake having orgasms."

"Oh," she said as if the whole inquiry were just beginning to make sense to her. "Why . . . always."

"Always . . . ?"

"Yes. Always."

"Oh God . . ."

Sally shrugged her shoulders, closed the cap on her jar of lotion, got into bed, put on her glasses, opened her copy of Vidal's *Burr*, and commenced to read with apparent absorption. Can you feature that? The bloodless gall? In case you're having trouble, let me just run this back for you: my wife of five and a half years has just told me that every single act of love between us was a staged event, mummery, a fake. Then, her message sent and received, she plotzes down to read a book. You'd think we had been talking about the weather, or Nixon or Elmer Fudd. Her behavior seemed so doggedly indifferent to what should have been any reasonable person's apprehension of seriousness, that I wondered if one of us was crazy, really crazy. And since I was the one most upset, I wondered if it was me. The whole room started taking on a hallucinatory glow.

Would I have felt better if Sally collapsed in my arms and sobbed her heart out from the years of accumulated grief? Or if she bellowed like a madwoman and accused me of multiple crimes against her body and spirit?

Perhaps in expecting something more, expecting something different, I was expecting her to not be Sally. But being Sally, she acted as if to trifle over something as mundane as our sex life was really asking too much. In a way, it was a throwback to her attitude about abortions, or being shipped off to prep school: just another thing she "didn't mind." It was as if she just handed me a ticking bomb and casually said, "Here, I don't need this, you take it   and then walked away without looking back to notice if my head was blown off. Call it an act of obtuseness, of omission, commission, bad manners, sadism stupidity, calculation . . . ? It struck me as a performance of the purest contempt.

Whether she truly felt anything under that mask of indifference I will never know. If she was moved, or shaken if she thought the whole thing was secretly hilarious, I can't tell you. She sure didn't show it. It is true of course, that I made no attempt to reach out to her at this point, whether she requested it or not. To comfort her To tell her it was all right.

It wasn't all right. I felt like she slammed a door in my face

Things were spinning in a centrifugal whirl of confusion I remember saying something vapid and idiotic like 'We're going to have to do something about this, Sally   Then, I got up, put on my clothes and staggered out of the house. I walked around outside for a long time, aimlessly traversing the campus. There was a lot of noise in the dorm clusters—kids making new friends at the beginning of the school year, loud rock 'n' roll booming out of the windows. The happy commotion of these kids compared with my own collapsing, nerveless existence filled me with an emotion which I immediately recognized as self pity, and lacking even the nerve to shuck it off felt all the more pitiable. Eventually, I returned to the house and slept curled up in the rug in front of the fireplace like a dog

The next morning, I called Bob Krock and begged him to meet me that afternoon for a drink. He said "sure" and suggested this bar down in the village. He could tell that something was wrong but was evidently satisfied to wait a few hours and find out what it was. My two classes that day survive in my memory as sort of a cataleptic blur—tears once dampening my cheeks during some introductory remarks about Hawthorne. The afternoon class, a Thoreau seminar, I dismissed early.

The Old Sawmill was a cinder block cube attached to a supermarket in a shopping center. The inside of the bar was a strange confusion of styles, sort of a Las Vegas–Mafia evocation of New England rusticity. The lower half of the walls was wormy wood wainscoting. Above this was wallpaper with cubist renditions of cows, roosters and other barely recognizable barnyard creatures. There were a few antique tools hung on the walls. Each table had a patio candle covered with plastic netting. The bar was padded with a Naugahyde-covered cushion which was pockmarked with shiny craters from cigarette burns. Bob was late. By the time he arrived I had already put away two Black Russians. Even though it was dim in there, I think he could see from my reddened eyes that I had been crying.

"Hey, what's up, buddy?"

"I hate this fucking place," I said, and started blubbering.

"What—?"

"All this plastic bullshit."

"You want to go somewhere else?"

"No."

You could tell that Bob was already having a hard time with my histrionics. He looked furtively around the place to see if anyone we knew was there, but there were only a couple of car-dealer types at the bar. The bartender was absorbed in polishing some glasses, and in the back room two waitresses were setting up for the dinner hour. Finally, he swung his battered old briefcase onto a nearby stool, arranged his Marlboros and Zippo lighter on the bar, took off his jacket, and sat down. He whistled to get the bartender's attention, and the car dealers turned their heads.

"What are you drinking?" he asked me.

"I dunno. Black Russians."

"What the fuck you drinking that kind of stuff for?"

"I dunno. Just am."

"A Miller's, please," he told the bartender, "and a Black Russian for my, uh, friend here."

The bartender went down to his well to mix it. The car dealers resumed their conversation. When Bob was satisfied that no one was looking at us anymore, he said, "What the hell's the matter with you?"

"Sally never had an orgasm. She's been faking it for more than five years." I started quietly blubbering again. The bartender brought us our drinks. I finished up the old one and took a swallow of the fresh one.

"What was that?" Bob said.

"You heard me."

Bob drew in his breath sharply, gave a quick shake of the head, and exhaled. He poured his beer into a glass. "Gosh," he said, as if at a loss, "how do you like that?"

"What am I gonna do?"

"Do . . . ? How long's this been goin' on?"

"I told you, over five years!"

"Okay, okay. Calm down, huh. Drink your drink."

"Sure could have fooled me. Five and a half years."

"What, did you just find out, or what?"

"Last night."

"She told you last night? Mentioned it or something?"

"Yeah."

"And you didn't know?"

I looked up at him and shook my head. He just whistled and shook his head slightly. "Maybe you ought to see a shrink or something?" he said after a while.

"Me? She's the one."

"Yeah, I know. But maybe if you both went or something."

"Are you kidding? She'd never go. Doesn't believe in it. Why, you know somebody?"

Bob mentioned Chesmire. He was up Route 7 in Arlington. Bob had seen him for a few months several years earlier, he said, over some personal problem. He said Chesmire was "real good."

"I'll give him a call," I said. "Maybe."

"It'd probably help."

"Yeah, I know," I said, and started sniffling again.

"Come on, Richie, cut that out. There's people—"

"I can't help it."

"Then change seats with me, will you?"

We changed seats so that I could face the corner and nobody would see what an asshole I was and Bob wouldn't be embarrassed in my company.

"Hey, you know you're not the only guy in the world who ever had a problem like—"

"It's not my problem! It's hers," I said vehemently.

"Yeah, well, okay, fine. Only don't go doin' anything foolish in the meantime."

"What would I do?"

"I'm not sayin' you'd *do* anything—"

"Yes you are. You just said, 'don't go doing anything—'"

"I didn't mean . . . ah shit. You know what I mean. I'm sayin' it's not the end of the world."

He was getting pretty frustrated with me, I could tell. And what's more, I think I was doing it on purpose, taking out my anger on him because I didn't have the guts the night before to take it out on Sally, where it belonged. So, I gave the guy a lot of credit for just putting up with me and my stupid bullshit.

"Look," he continued earnestly, "they have all kinds

of knowledge in the psychiatric field that they didn't have even ten years ago. You know: Masters and Johnson, all sorts of stuff. You two take yourselves up to this shrink, Chesmire, and work it out."

"I told you, she'll never go."

"Then go yourself. It can't hurt you."

"No. I suppose not."

"And hey, think about it this way: it didn't hurt you any all those years *not* knowin' about it, right?"

"What . . . ?"

"About them orgasms."

"So . . . ?"

"So, why go batshit now?"

"Casuistry."

"What . . . ?"

"Forget it."

"It's just common sense, Rich."

"I know. I know. I'm such an asshole I can't believe it."

"You're not an asshole. You just got to get yourself together and realize the sky's not fallin'."

"I will, I swear."

"Good. And stop drinkin' them Black Russians."

"I will."

"And call this shrink."

"I'll call him."

"Now you're talkin'," Bob said and ordered another beer for himself. He did not order me another Black Russian, which was just as well because I was starting to see double. We just sat there for a long time not saying anything. The bar was filling up now. The patrons were nearly all men, small-down dandies in doubleknits, probably real-estate salesmen, dentists, insurance agents, men who inhabited a different Reddington than the fools and dreamers up on the mountain. I wondered how many of them had problems with their wives and guessed a lot of them. It was no particular consolation to arrive at this conclusion. I stirred my drink with a finger.

"Sally's been acting a little crazy for a while now," I said. "I don't know what's eating her. Maybe she's bored not having a job or something. I dunno. She's constantly belittling me for no reason at all. Picking fights. She acts so goddamned superior all the time."

"Did you ask her if somethin' was buggin' her?"

"Sort of. Yes."

"And what'd she say?"

"One thing you don't do is ask Sally a simple question and expect to get a straight answer. She's a real aficionada of the mental Chinese fire drill."

"The old head-fuck game, huh?"

"You bet."

"Well, that's a little sick right there."

"Sick? I dunno. But it's sure not too helpful."

"That's why I think a shrink would really pay off in your situation. Unclog lines of communications, to start with."

"Would you do me a favor?"

Bob shrugged his shoulders. He looked at me expectantly for a moment.

"What?" he said.

"You know how Sally and Annie are always hanging around together?"

"Yeah . . . ?"

"They must talk about us, sex, you know, their lives."

"I imagine they do."

"Maybe you can find out from Annie what's bugging Sally."

"Ask her yourself."

"No. I really couldn't."

"Why not?"

"I . . . I just don't know her well enough. I mean,

Sally's the one who's her friend. If I approached her about this I'd look like a sneaky, conniving bastard. Just do me a favor and probe around a little and see what you come up with."

Bob said he'd give it a try. Someone put a quarter in the jukebox and an uproar of Motown jive filled the room. We left immediately.

You know the details of my first meeting with Chesmire, his ridicule of the way I presented my "problem," my decision to not walk out the door. Anyway, near the end of that session I did come clean and tell Chesmire and the group about Sally faking her orgasms. I just sort of mentioned it during the final minutes when time was already up. Chesmire said it would help a lot if Sally joined me in therapy. I said I'd ask her, but added I wasn't too optimistic.

Can you guess what her answer was? I'm sure you can imagine the general drift, though not the level of charm and wit. She told me to blow it out my ass. She said they'd hold the Winter Olympics in hell before she "subjected" herself to some psychiatrist's couch—shows how much *she* knew.

I tried to reassure her that there wasn't any couch. I explained that it was group therapy. What a mistake.

"Oh!" she bellowed. "That's even better. Strip myself naked in front of a bunch of strangers, huh? A bunch of . . . of *sickies* no less."

"They're just ordinary people with ordinary problems."

"Bully for them. I'll pass, if you don't mind."

"Do you have any suggestions of your own, then? You know a better way to address this problem?"

"What problem?" Sally said.

A few days later I saw Chesmire again and reported Sally's answer about joining the group. He listened and then suggested that maybe it wasn't a problem for Sally after all, since she didn't perceive it as a problem.

"It's a problem for me, though," I said.

"I can see that it is."

"So, if she won't come here, what do I do? Just forget it?"

"You can."

"Get serious."

"Richard, life is largely a matter of what you pay attention to. What you choose to pay attention to."

"Great. So you want me to pretend that nothing happened, that everything's normal, and resume my regular married life?"

"*I* don't want you to do anything. What's important is what you want to do."

"I want my wife to be okay."

"How are you going to do that?"

"I don't know—get her to have orgasms."

"Uh-huh. How are you going to do that?"

"I don't know. Find some way to . . . to make her."

"You can't make her have anything she doesn't want to have."

"So, what am I going to do?"

"Consider alternatives."

"Like what?"

"Maybe it's time you quit trying to make her have what she doesn't want to have."

"Maybe. But ultimately we can't keep on having a marriage under those conditions."

"Perhaps not," Chesmire said.

It was an idea that I was not really prepared to entertain, that I hadn't entertained consciously, that is, until the words left my mouth. And hearing it from my own mouth, and then Chesmire agreeing, left me momentarily stricken with nausea. I thought of Sally back in Washington, the smashingly pretty girl at the Tidal Basin. Of Sally in New York, braving the deadly streets. Of Sally in Cambridge, my Country maiden, sharer of my Country dreams.

"Maybe what you need to do is concentrate on yourself, on your own act, instead of requiring somebody else to behave a certain way, to live up to conditions set by you," Chesmire said. "You see, that's the trouble with a desire to control other people, to make them do what *you* want. In the final analysis, the person you exercise the most complete control over is . . . yourself. You'd be amazed at what you can get yourself to do, as opposed to the difficulty of getting other people to do what you want. This is another secret of human existence," Chesmire said. An incandescent smile was visible through his full beard, not a smug or self-satisfied expression, as it might appear, but one of expansive and genuine delight. I just stared back blankly, however, still stunned by my prospects for the future.

"Tell me, Richard," he continued. "Is there something you can think of that you can do for yourself that doesn't require you to change somebody else, or persuade them to act according to your wishes and values?"

"Whu . . . ?" I croaked. My head was spinning and I felt as if I was going to break down and bawl any second. "I don't know," I finally answered his question. "I'll have to think about it.

"Fine," Chesmire said, then directed his attention to the others. "Does anybody else want to work?" This was his jargon meaning would anybody else care to discuss their particular problems. One of the women began discussing her marriage. She was the one I have described previously—not a bad-looking specimen of the common housewife with a rather robust figure and not the greatest taste in clothes—she was partial to pantsuits. Finally, there was the question of her black eye.

She had been married for fifteen years to some character named Don who slugged her when he got drunk, which was getting to be more and more often as the years wore on. Don was general manager of a manufacturing concern in Rutland that produced sporting and camping footwear. Obviously Gloria and Don's marriage was going nowhere fast, but Gloria could not really see beyond three alternative courses of action: 1) kill herself; 2) kill Don; or 3) kill herself and Don. As you can see, she was somewhat stuck in the realm of extremes. What Gloria decided, as far as this particular week was concerned, was to stay home and continue to be slapped around by Don until a better idea came along.

Chesmire said this was "fine" as long as Gloria was willing to "take responsibility" for the decision.

Next, a fat woman complained about being fat and about how loathsome she was and how there was nothing she could do about it. All her diets were failures. She always regained the weight she lost. She lacked the discipline to exercise. She was a lost cause.

Chesmire agreed that she was fat. He told her to eat even more than she was already eating, to give up trying to stick to her diets.

She said he was crazy.

He said that this was indeed a possibility.

She called him "a sadist."

Chesmire said he wasn't responsible for her getting fat and maintaining herself in that condition, and whether or not he seemed to be a sadist or not had nothing whatsoever to do with her weight problem.

The fat woman started to cry, big drooling sobs.

The first woman, Don's punching bag, Gloria, told her to cut it out. Voices were raised until there was considerable screaming. Chesmire announced that the group's time was up.

"Wait," I said. "I've been thinking it over and I believe I can answer your question now."

"Good for you. Save it for next time."

"Can't I tell you now?"

"No," Chesmire said. "I've had enough of you assholes for one day."

The term, *asshole*, I would learn was Chesmire's favorite term of endearment. Anyway, driving back to Reddington that evening, the *idea*, in all its ramifications, grew clearer and clearer in my mind. And it also dawned on me that I did not need Chesmire's "permission" to go ahead and act on my idea. That itself was uplifting.

seven

So, what was this fabulous idea? Did I decide to lock Sally in the basement until she starved or had the required orgasm? Or possibly kill her, stuff her body in the septic tank, then take off and commence the life of a beachcomber in the Cayman Islands, to dine on plantains and violate the simple, brown-skinned native girls till they squealed for mercy? Or buy a Great Dane puppy and train him to service Sally until blood ran out of her ears and her obdurate loins ached with passion and pleasure?

Obviously none of these abominations. Then why do I even mention them? Just to give you a feeling for the rather weird latitudes my thinking was drifting into around that time. I was getting a little warped—but I was still too civilized a fellow to *carry through* anything really drastic.

No, my fabulous idea was really quite simple and harmless: I resolved to get my body into shape. That's all. I reasoned that physical fitness was the first step on the road back to self-esteem, and best of all here was a plan that did not require the participation or approval or persuasion of others. The result would certainly be increased well-being, poise, self-possession, and the ability to cope with the world at large.

I am five feet, ten inches tall and weigh 160 pounds. But, at the time that concerns us here I weighed something like 190. Yes, I was getting tubby. It was awful. I mean, I didn't look all that bad with clothes on, but naked it was possible to see all the ravages of the sedentary life teaming up with time and gravity to spread me on the surface of the Earth like vanilla pudding. These were the horrible consequences of ten years spent in the seated position, on my ass in classrooms, offices, libraries, cars, in front of televisions, in restaurants. It's amazing how it just sneaks up on you.

Each morning in the bathroom had become a horrifying moment of truth. The mirror was my nemesis, the image in it a leering, mocking caricature of young manhood. My pectoral muscles, once squarish plates like the body armor of a Roman legionnaire, had shrunk to mere fleshy cones, almost teat-like from inactivity. Below this was a paunch, a roll, a spare tire, a ring of flab that resembled one of those foam belts worn around the waist by water-skiers. My arms, once meaty engines from endless games of high school basketball, the swim team, tennis, and even bench-pressing, were now more like whitened stalks of vegetable matter. My legs seemed hardly adequate to the task of traversing the distance between one chair and another, pale, spindly, unappealing.

It was the terrible paleness, the cadaverlike semi-translucency of my skin, which frightened me the most. I was twenty-nine—if you put a paper bag over my head and placed me on a police lineup, I might have passed for fifty-nine. A shapeless bag of tallow. It was awful.

It wasn't always like this. In fact, I had the snapshots to prove it.

Exhibit A: myself on the beach at Amagansett circa 1966, probably age seventeen. I am wearing cutoff jeans. There is a surfboard stuck on end in the sand to my right. I am as lean and as bronze as Frankie Avalon in *Beach Blanket Bingo,* notwithstanding the poor picture quality. The photo brings tears to my eyes—not that I'm completely narcissistic, but it was like seeing a photo of someone you were once very fond of who is now dead and gone.

Exhibit B: myself again, perhaps four summers later. Sally and I are on the courts at Dad's racquet club. I am frozen in mid-backswing, playing with complete authority, so handsome in my whites, tendons standing out like piano wires in my neck as I reach for the ball (while Sally, my doubles partner, stands agog to my left—erect nipples showing slyly through the thin fabric of her little outfit). Yes, these are the kind of healthy young people who are irresistibly drawn together as lovers, fine, young, healthy, lusty specimens at their reproductive peaks!

And then, a few years later? I am afraid to look at my own image in the bathroom mirror. I would make it a point to shave *after* I was through with my shower, when the mirror was all steamed up and I could accomplish the task by wiping a hole just big enough to see my face in, the horror of my limbs and torso happily obscured.

You see, in an attempt to Be-Honest-With-Myself, I had to consider that the condition of my body was *The Problem* between me and Sally after all. She probably no longer found me attractive. And, honestly, after a long hard look at the corpus delicti, who could blame her? I was a mess. I had to admit it. A lot of guys my age were in even worse shape than myself—a lot worse shape. In fact, I saw them all the time: men in their twenties, bald, fat, stooped, wheezing. But, so what if others were worse off? It didn't mitigate my problem. No, I had to admit it: the way I had come to look probably turned Sally off. It was painful, but probably true. Especially when I thought about the old days back at G.W.U. where I was quite the amateur jock, what with my regular weekly game of hoop with the guys, my tennis, those weekends on the slopes of the nearby Blue Ridge, those happy afternoons spent Frisbeeing with my beloved golden retriever, Roscoe, now sadly deceased. Back then, I stayed in shape. Ruin followed. I played a little squash with Krezney at Harvard. After that, my daily exercise dwindled to shifting gears on a Volvo. Pathetic.

From the shoulders up, at least, the years had been kinder. My curly, almost kinky, straw-colored hair was perhaps a little thinner on top, the brow a little higher, but what was left seemed to be rooted pretty firmly. I wore it kind of long and bushy, like Art Garfunkel on the Simon and Garfunkel albums.

My straight nose with its dozen or so freckles, its thin, sensitive nostrils, was my best feature. The way things were going, I was lucky it hadn't turned black and fallen off. For years I wore a bushy carrot-colored moustache under it—at least until that last year of school, when I shaved it for the job interviews. The eyes were blue, kind eyes, perhaps credulous eyes at their worst, but not a trace of meanness in them. My chin could have been a little bolder, perhaps, a little squarer, but what the hell, you can't have everything. I was satisfied with the face. It was the body that went with it that gave me the creeps.

And so, you see, I made up my mind to take corrective measures. This was my program:

Always a strong swimmer (competitively in high school), I decided to make that excellent activity the mainstay of my daily routine. I aimed for 2,000 yards, seventy-two laps, roughly a mile. This would be augmented four times a week with some moderate weight-lifting. Finally, I decided to add a morning jog—nothing outlandish, mind you, just a couple of miles around the bosky lanes of the campus.

Creating the program in my head and on paper was rather easier than *doing* it. My first night in the pool was incredibly demoralizing. I could barely finish ten consecutive laps before groping for the gutter. My attempt at two lengths of "fly" left me croaking like a gaffed dogfish. I did not make a third of my goal that first night, and even so, the rest-stops were numerous. But hell, only a fool would expect Olympic times after a twelve-year retirement. And though my performance that first night was a tad discouraging, I did not let it get me down. In a week I was covering my 1,000 yards freestyle without stopping. At about sixteen minutes, I was getting down to a reasonable pace. To this I was able to add 200 yards of sloppy "fly." The rest was breaststroke and kickboard work. The jogging, alas, I dispensed with after three days. It was simply too punishing at seven o'clock in the morning. I rather enjoyed the weight-lifting and looked forward to its mindless repetitions before my swim. After ten days, I started to notice some results. I no longer resembled a garden slug.

Did any of this help me win back hard-hearted Sally? Hmmmm . . . Not if you take her behavior as the best evidence. Actually, our relationship began to take surrealistic detours. We continued to live together, of course, but with no acknowledgment that anything significant had happened, that anything had altered the parameters of our marriage. We were simply not communicating. It was really eerie.

For example, our paths crossed in the morning, but I would read a book over my Product 19 while Sally puttered around watering the plants with the *Today Show* in the background. She stopped cooking dinner for me in the evenings in any formal sense. I would come home and find her steaming up hellish porridges of brown rice, tofu and tamari. She was going "organic" all of a sudden. "Want some?" she would ask, kind of offhandedly. I would politely decline and put a frozen Weight Watchers dinner in the Toaster Oven. You see, part of the surrealistic aspect of all this was that our mutual behavior was undergoing a weird sort of devolution. The scene I have just described, for instance, would have been common back in our Columbia days, when we were too exhausted physically to talk most of the time. But supposedly we were beyond that. We were civilized now. Obviously, it was all a device to avoid or discourage communication, as if we both needed time to work out some dogged problem. But what, exactly, was being worked out?

Meanwhile there was our bizarre bedroom life. We continued to sleep in the same bed, oh, for weeks and weeks after the Big Rift. Do you see how unconscious we were? Zombies. I suppose I stupidly harbored the hope that she would notice how sleek my body was getting after all that swimming and pumping iron. I strutted around the room naked, flexing slyly when I thought she was looking. I strutted in vain.

Then, one gruesome night when I couldn't take it any longer, I jumped her from behind and took her by main force. She was lying on her side in bed with her back to me when I did it. She was reading. She did not close her book while I thrust and moaned.

"Didja feel that?" I asked her, panting, when I was done.

"Feel what?"

"Feel my prick fucking you."

"Is that what that was?"

"Yes."

"I thought it was my yeast infection. It's been itching like crazy all day."

What a comedian! How droll. I ripped one of the

fucking blankets off the bed and stormed into the other room where *Honniker's Progress* languished beside the typewriter. Our backpacking equipment was stored there and I blew up one of the air mattresses. It must have begun to occur to me that we couldn't go on living like that.

When I described the evolving domestic situation to Chesmire he observed that it was indeed an ominous arrangement.

"If I only knew why this was all happening . . ." I said to him and the group.

"Richard," he replied, "things happen or they don't happen. *Why* is irrelevant. Without any *whys* the whole universe would continue just as it is. *Why* is a diversion. *Why* is a waste of time. *Why* is a dead end. You have got to give up all of these *whys* and deal with what *is*."

"But why . . . ?"

Then, I met Dudley.

Yes, Dudley. No, not a little blonde-haired Protestant schoolboy. Not a sheep either. Far from it. Do you think that all the humiliation and frustration of dealing with Sally was turning me into a child molester? A humper of livestock?

Dudley was a girl. No, check that. Dudley was a woman. No, check that too. Dudley was a sort of *bouquet garni* of hormones wrapped up in the body of a woman with the mind of a willful little girl. As things turned out, she had been in one of my freshman comp classes since the beginning of the semester, but being a zombie fuckhead, and what with jumping through Sally's hoop and being under somewhat of a strain, shall we say, since classes began, I had failed to notice her—how, I don't know.

Anyway, it was one night during my swim in the

college pool. I was halfway down the lane in my fortieth lap when we collided in the water. You see, swimming laps one's mind tends to drift. I was not paying attention to where I was going because I understood that the lane I was occupying was mine alone for that hour. So I did not expect another body to be in the space. The instant following the moment of impact, I let her have it. I didn't know who she was, naturally, and I didn't wait to find out. To me, she was just some shithead who failed to observe the protocol of the pool and provoked my wrath as a result. I called her names and asked her just where the fuck she thought she was swimming and told her to stay the fuck out of *my* lane and swim in her own. I mean, obviously it was an over-reaction. I had so much hostility and anger brewing inside of me from the dismal march of recent events that it just spilled over onto her, like the breaking of one of those earthen dams in Appalachia that bring devastation to innocents in the valley below. She hauled off and slugged me.

"Don't you yell at me, you fuckin' creep!" she screamed and then socked me again. She really landed a good one, right on the chin. Luckily, we were in the shallow end of the pool, because she really rang my bell. All of a sudden I felt my legs go all rubbery, and the next moment my head was bobbing up and down in the water, where I heard additional and fragmentary imprecation; ". . . pig-fucker . . .", ". . . free pool . . .", "lousy manners . . .", ". . . maniac . . ."

I was too stunned to say anything after that. Soon the lifeguard came over and told us to break it up and asked what the hell was going on. I just mumbled something about my proprietory rights and resumed my laps. Luckily, they didn't throw me out of the pool. (Luckily, the incident wasn't reported to Dean Lansing.)

When I was done with my laps, about fifteen minutes later, I crawled off to the sauna to bake out all the rage and meanness that was festering away inside of me, that was, in fact, beginning to frighten me as I became aware of it and how it was affecting my behavior. It was ten o'clock. The gym was going to close in a half an hour. The idea of returning to the house depressed me even more than usual. Anyway, I was alone in the sauna, reading a three-week-old copy of *Newsweek* when the girl entered through the redwood door. She was wrapped in a lavender towel. It took me a moment to recognize her without her bathing cap. She glared at me hatefully for a moment, then climbed up to the slatted shelf above where I sat. We just sat there silently for a few minutes. Finally, I apologized.

"That was awfully rude of me out there in the pool. I'm sorry I yelled at you."

"It sure was rude. It was just as much your fault that we crashed."

"Ah—"

"You weren't looking where you were going."

"You realize that you were in my lane . . . ?"

"It's not *your* damn lane. You act like you own it or something. Well, you don't!"

"I consider it mine during the half hour or so that I'm using it. There is such a thing as common sense, you know. If you're using the barbells, someone doesn't come over and stand on them while you want to use them. You—"

"It's not the same thing. How can you compare barbells and a pool. One's a *thing*, and one's a *space*. That's stupid!"

"Okay, but you could try swimming lengthwise instead of crosswise, like everybody else."

"Look, you have your way and I have mine."

"Fine, but if you swim crossways, you're asking for trouble."

"What makes you think that your way's the only way?"

"There are lines painted on the bottom. The goddam

lines run lengthwise. Did you notice that? And that's the way I was swimming, lengthwise."

"So?"

"So, obviously that's the way you're supposed to swim!"

"Is that a fact?"

"Yes, it is a goddam fa-fa-fa—" I turned around to make my final point about the lanes and saw that she was naked.

"Hey, you're Dr. Schuster!"

"I whu—"

"I'm in your English class. Comp and lit. You don't look the same with your hair all wet and scraggly."

"I—"

I also probably didn't look the same with my eyes bugging out and my jaw hanging down to my lap. She was amazingly beautiful. You could see the tan marks from her bikini. Her breasts and hips were a cream color, while the rest of her was copper, like one of those Brazilian beach bunnies. She had long black hair. Her snatch hair was also black, naturally, and her nipples were very dark, heavily pigmented. Like almost all Reddington girls, she was immaculately groomed. Her fingernails and toenails were painted chocolate brown, the same color as her nipples. She couldn't have acted more casual about her nudity. Because she was in my freshman comp class, I realized that she was no more than eighteen and possibly even seventeen years old. The idea made my head spin. I wondered what kind of a home could produce such a brazen, beautiful child. It was marvelous and horrifying. I, of course, still had my soggy old trunks on.

"You *are* Dr. Schuster, aren't you?"

"Uh, uhga . . . uh, yes . . ."

"Well, I'm in your class!"

"You are?"

"Yes. Dudley Roper? You don't recognize me, do you?"

"Dugha . . . Duh . . ."

"God, it must be a zillion degrees in here. I have to go now." She wrapped herself back up in the towel and climbed down from her seat. "I'm sorry I punched you, but you were so nasty, you didn't even give me a second to say I'm sorry out there."

"I flew off the handle. I've been under a strain. I'm sorry I yelled at you."

She stood there for another moment right in front of me, the sweat glistening on her face and shoulders.

"Well, see you in English," she said and left.

I sat there for about another five minutes. The crinkled old *Newsweek* was on my lap, right over the lump in my swimming trunks. Somewhere outside the sauna, I thought I heard animal noises, distant screechings, barks and howls, and I wondered what they were.

She was there, all right, in my one o'clock comp and lit class the next day. Why hadn't I noticed this stunning creature (who called herself Dudley, for reasons that are probably only comprehensible to a teenager from Ridgefield, Connecticut—in spite of the fact that her legal name was *Alice* Dudley Roper).

Why hadn't I noticed any of the others? Of the fifteen freshmen in my class (not counting the two boys) at least half of them were definitely attractive and only one was an outright disaster.

I mean, I must have realized they were *there*, taking up space. But as females, as sexual entities, as warm, live bodies? Forget it. Up until the moment of Dudley's blasé striptease in the sauna, I was out-to-lunch, a zombie, among the walking dead. Also, of course, a married man with hopes and dreams and circumscribed lusts.

But suddenly, it had all changed overnight. Though

Dudley was clearly the bombshell of the group, I couldn't keep my eyes off their chests, off their asses as they milled around before class. A crazy idea came to me of locking the classroom door, raping all the pretty ones in sequence, and being dragged of to the Vermont state penitentiary to be castrated and gassed—but you already know the extreme directions my fantasy life was veering in.

Sweat was breaking out on my upper lip, and my hands started to tremble as Bob Krock's words of over a year ago came back into my head: ". . . you'll be just like a little kid in a candy store . . ."

All of a sudden I noticed that the students had all quieted down and were looking toward me with expectation for the class to begin. I tried to blink my way out of the trance and soon I was able to apprehend reality again. I reached for my battered copy of *Walden* and began reading passages from the beginning of Thoreau's opening chapter, "Economy."

I read out loud with the facility of one who once nourished foolish hopes for a career on the stage (high school). But it was something I could carry off semi-consciously, daydreaming meanwhile about disembodied sex organs, lips, asses, vulvas. I had read maybe three or four pages, just through the paragraph about men leading lives of quiet desperation, when I stopped. The reason I stopped was because I was imagining what it would be like to fuck Sally with an enormous zucchini, and the obvious hostility behind this idle thought made me break out sweating again.

"That's heavy," a girl in the front said.

"Whu . . . ?"

"I mean, like, those are, like, heavy thoughts."

"What?"

"What he's saying about people's lives, like."

"What's your name?"

"Bethy Wilson."

"Bethy, did you finish high school?"

"Yes. Only it was, like, a private school, you know, not a regular high school."

"I see. But you did graduate?"

"Oh, yeah sure."

"Then how come you can't speak English?"

Poor Bethy was too stunned to answer my mean question. The others in the class tittered behind her back, as if they were glad to see the eager beaver get shot down for trying to brown-nose the teacher. Dudley was not among the titterers, I noticed.

"No, seriously Bethy, that's an interesting observation. Shall we continue . . . ?"

I was mean and nasty for the rest of the day. I made fun of my students' vocabularies, their accents, ridiculed their enthusiastic comments, and generally acted like a small-minded little shit. It was a bad performance. I was using my emotions like Jimmy Cagney with a sawed-off shotgun, just blasting anyone who dared to rub me the wrong way. I was out of control. I figured by the end of the day the registrar would be swamped with requests to drop my courses. And the whole time I kept on hearing these crazy jungle noises. At first, I thought it was the squirrels outside the classroom. Soon, it occurred to me that I was really losing my marbles.

That night, I was up in the office at home trying to work on *Honniker's Progress*. After reading over the chapter I had, I realized that the steel mill was all wrong. The whole goddam thing had to go—twenty-four pages of melodramatic drivel. Eventually, I decided to shift the scene to a wheat farm in North Dakota, a poetic setting that would underscore the forces of loneliness and abandonment that form and *deform* the adult Honniker later on. I had just gotten him to the point of puberty when the phone rang.

Sally answered it downstairs. She yelled up that it was for me. I took the call in what I was coming to think of as *"her"* bedroom—since I had spent about a week sleeping in the spare room.

"Hello . . ."

"Dr. Schuster?"

"Yes—?"

"Hi. This is Dudley Roper."

"Dudly Ro—"

"From your comp class."

"Oh, uh, hi Dudley . . ." My stomach was suddenly one big knot. I lit a cigarette, but as I took the first drag that thing happened where the cigarette accidently gets glued to your lips and as you pull your hand away the goddam thing slides through your fingers and the red-hot ash at the end burns the fuck out of your hand.

"What did you say?"

"Nothing Dudley. I just . . . dropped the phone for a second there—"

"Are you going to the pool tonight?" she asked.

"I dunno, yes, I guess so, maybe."

"Does that mean you'll be there?" She sounded like she was giggling.

"Uh, Dudley, there's something about me that I don't think you understand."

"What?"

I was about to spell it out for her when it occurred to me that she understood perfectly well that I was married. She must have known that. They print your wife's name right next to yours in the little telephone directory that the college puts out for students and faculty. At the very least, she must've been suspicious when Sally answered the phone. But notice it didn't deter her!

"What don't I understand? I was just wondering if you were going to the pool."

"Nothing, Dudley. Yes, as a matter of fact I was planning to, uh, swim a few laps later."

"Oh. Okay."

"Why . . . ?" I asked.

"I was just wondering," she said. "Maybe I'll see you down there."

"Yes, sure, maybe."

"Okay, bye . . . ."

"Bye, Dudley."

I hung up, sat on the bed for a minute or so, then padded back into the office wondering whatever that was all about, as if I didn't have some inkling, as if I wasn't already giddy with excitement. What a jerk. Then, I heard footsteps on the stairway, a knock on the door.

"Come in."

Suddenly, I was leaning back in my chair, absolutely calm, poised, self-possessed—not counting the rather shit-eating grin I couldn't keep off my face.

"Who was that?" Sally inquired.

"Nobody," I said.

"It wasn't nobody."

"What do you think it was, then?"

"It was a woman," Sally said. "A young woman, probably a student."

"Correct," I said.

"What did she want?"

"What on Earth does it matter to you?"

"Don't play games with me, Richie. What was that all about?"

"She thought we were on-call."

"Oh really . . . ?"

"Her car won't start."

"You going to go over and help her start it?"

"Sally . . ." I started making these tsk-tsking sounds with my tongue. Sally glared at me for a moment, a really hateful, incandescently hostile look, then turned around and stormed out of the little room, slamming the door behind her.

A few minutes later I walked downstairs. She was sitting in the living room, pretending to look through the L.L. Bean catalog. Gerald R. Ford was on television, with the sound turned off. A Leonard Cohen album was on the stereo.

I grabbed my down vest from the rack beside the door and slipped it over my shirt.

"Feeling blue tonight?" I asked.

She just glared at me again. Her eyes were like little blue lasers. Otherwise, she didn't reply.

"That record you're listening to can't be much help," I said.

"Fuck you," she said.

Do I have to rehearse the details of my first adventure in adultery with that five-foot-three bundle of wantonness, Dudley Roper—how she blew me in the sauna, how she lured me back to her room in the old reconstructed village, how I gluttonized her fabulous body, like a hyena snorfling over the carcass of a young gazelle, how I humped and hollered until the dawn's early light, how she groaned, squawked, squealed and bellowed for more, and how I gave her more?

In the pink light of daybreak, then, we were disposed across her bed at right angles, myself still browsing hungrily in that nourishing shrub between her nut-brown, silky-smooth legs.

"Sometimes," she said, "you just want to come and come and come and never stop coming."

I agreed that this was so, not necessarily in plain English. Eventually, I had to withdraw my head from the unquenchable organ. My tongue ached. I pulled myself up to the headboard, threw my left arm around her, and collapsed with a moan of exhaustion against a pillow.

"You were awful in class yesterday," she said.

"Whu . . . ?"

"With Bethy."

"Bethy . . . ?"

"She's practically my best friend."

"Oh: Bethy."

"She thinks you're a monster."

"I don't know what got into me yesterday."

"I bet I do."

"Really . . . ?"

"Your wife."

I drew my arm out from under her neck and rolled over so I could see her.

"What about my wife?"

"Your marriage is going down the tubes."

"What do you know about it?"

"That it's going down the tubes."

"Well, I'm having some problems but— where did you get this information?"

"It's not important."

"It is to me. This happens to be rather personal, you know."

"I know," Dudley agreed. But unable to suppress a giggle, she tried to stifle it by putting the edge of the sheet in her mouth, like a little girl who dimly senses the shabbiness of laughing at the wrong thing, such as another's misery.

"I'd still like to know who told you my marriage was going down the tubes."

"No one," she insisted.

"And what if it wasn't like you said?"

"Would you be here if it wasn't?"

*   *   *

I left Dudley's place on Luxury Row at about nine that morning and headed back to the house to take a shower before my ten o'clock class. Without a wink of sleep, my head felt like a hollow gourd infested with weevils. There was a kind of continuous ringing sound in my ears like the beating of tiny wings. It was otherwise a dazzling autumn morning, the leaves blazing orange and scarlet and a high, clear, cloudless sky above.

Sally was sitting at the kitchen table, smoking a cigarette, which at that hour was rare for her, being an exceedingly light smoker, and then usually only when she was drinking. She did not, however, seem to be drinking now—at least nothing stronger than English breakfast tea. She did not seem in a good humor, either.

"Where were you last night?" she asked.

I stared at her for a moment.

"None of your goddam business," I finally told her, then hung up my vest and headed upstairs. I realized I was trembling. But something about being able to say that made me feel great inside. She was hot on my heels, though.

"It is too my goddam business, buster," she said, her voice now reaching a definitely hysterical pitch. "You think this is some kind of hotel you can check in and out of whenever you feel like it?"

I was taking my clothes off in *"her"* bedroom, getting ready to take a shower.

"To tell you the truth, Sally, I don't know what the fuck this place is anymore. It sure doesn't feel much like home, though, if that's what you mean."

"And I suppose that's my fault?" she said.

I was flabbergasted.

"Don't just *suppose!*" I told her angrily, "You can count on it!"

"You prick!"

"Ho ho."

"You scumbag!"

"Would you mind letting me in the bathroom, Sal? I've got a ten o'clock."

I squeezed past her and shut the door to the can. She yanked it open once I was inside, so I grabbed the knob and pushed it shut again. Then I turned the lock. She pounded on the door and screamed for a while, but it was hard to make out what she was saying, especially with the water running. Eventually, the racket stopped. When I finally emerged from the bathroom, Sally was nowhere to be seen. I threw on a pair of Levis and a polo shirt and went back downstairs.

There were two suitcases sitting in the middle of the braided rug in the living room. Sally, meanwhile, was sitting next to the woodstove. She was slowly and methodically feeding white paper into it.

"Going somewhere?" I inquired, pointing to the luggage.

"No," she said. "You are."

Suddenly, and with a pang of horror, I realized that the white papers she was feeding to the fire were pages from the first chapter of *Honniker's Progress*.

"You vicious cunt!"

She looked up at me, grinning: a big smarmy smirk of satisfaction.

"Go ahead," I told her, "burn the fucking thing. It may interest you to know that I was going to take him off that wheat farm and start all over again anyway, so don't think you're hurting me. Here, I'll help you—"

I ripped the rest of the chapter away from her and chucked the whole damn thing in the stove myself.

"The story is in my head," I told her. "Try stuffing that in the stove!"

"Get out of here," she said. The smile, however phoney, was now gone from her face.

"Oh yeah? What if I refuse?"

"I'll call the police."

"I suppose they'll throw me out of my own house—"

"Of course they will, stupid."

She smirked again, really testing my anger.

"What if I want *you* out instead?" I said.

"No way, José. Pick up your bags and beat it."

"If you don't watch out, you're going to have a divorce on your hands."

"Funny, I was just about to mention that. I'm calling a lawyer myself this morning. I advise you to do the same. I'll tell you right now, Rich, I don't intend to punish you. You can keep your car, since it means so much to you. I'll take the rest."

"The rest . . . ?"

"Yes, of our joint possessions."

"You will, huh?"

"Unless you put up a fight. In which case I'll go for the car too."

"You vicious cunt!"

"You're repeating yourself."

"What makes you think you can stay here without me around? Huh? Does it occur to your little pea brain that this house is ours only by dint of my association with the college? This house is part of my salary!"

"Fine. Take your pick. You can have either the house or your salary."

"You're not going to get away with this, Sally."

"It's not a question of 'getting away with.'"

"They'll throw your ass right out of here."

"No they won't. The college will make arrangements. With the court."

"You vicious cunt!"

"You're beginning to sound like a broken record."

"You backstabbing twat!"

"Oh, a little variety—!"

"What if I stuff your fucking head in the wood-stove?"

"Then you will probably go to jail for a long, long time. Don't you have a ten o'clock?"

"Yeah—"

"Well, it's five after."

I glowered at her, then lurched over and picked up the suitcases.

"Don't think you're going to get away with this, Sally. You're not the only one who can get a lawyer! You're not the only one who can fight dirty! You better look for an apartment! You better make plans of your own!"

"Bye Bye, Rich. It's been nice talking to you."

I looked at her for a moment, then at all the things, the objects, around the room. A golden beam of morning sunlight was slanting through an east window. It seemed so pure and simple, like the dreams we shared for so many years.

"Just one thing I'd like to know, Sally: why is this all happening? When we finally have what we want here in this place?"

A wistful, faraway look suddenly glazed her eyes, as if she had retreated for a moment to a place in her brain where she could touch those happy memories of the dreams we shared. But a moment later, she sighed and then frowned.

"It's too complicated to go into just now," she said.

"But Sally, I love you."

"It's something you'll learn to get over. Others have."

"What!"

"Please, Rich. Go."

"What others?"

"It's not important, Rich. You're missing your class."

I threw my bags in the back seat of the old Volvo and took off.

First, I had to go over to the English department offices on the old town square and cancel my classes for the day. Then I hurried over to Bob Krock's house. He lived on the same winding road just off the campus as Mac MacWhorter, but Bob's place was a rather humdrum split-level suburban bunker.

Bob was not there, but Annie was home. I must have been acting pretty strangely because she looked a little confused and frightened. I asked her if I could use the phone. She showed me the phone in the kitchen.

"Is there an extension somewhere. I need something a little more private."

"There's one in Bob's study."

"Fine."

Oddly enough, I hadn't been in the house more than a half dozen times and didn't really know where things were. Most of the time, when we all hung around together, Bob and Annie came over to our place. Otherwise, Bob and I conducted the bulk of our friendship in bars, on trout streams, or in automobiles going to and from bars and trout streams.

Annie took me by the hand and led me into Bob's study. It was a dark bear's den of brown leather chairs and sofas and books. There were louvered shutters over the windows so that even during the day the room had an air of perpetual twilight—probably a required mood-setter for a poet like Bob. The shelves filled two entire walls and were crammed with volumes. At the center of this animal lair, this dark bear's den, was a huge, ornate mahogany desk. The phone was on the desk. Annie pointed it out to me and I sat down gingerly in the swivel chair. For some reason, sitting in that chair behind that huge desk gave you a feeling of immense power, which, as a matter of fact, came in very handy at that particular moment. Annie patted me on the hand and left me alone, shutting the door behind her.

I had to get a hold of Krezney, my old pal from Cambridge, now a member of the bar. We had been out of touch for about a year at that point, both of us rather slovenly in our approach to correspondence. I knew he was practicing in Boston, doing whatever young lawyers do when they start out in the profession. It was my feeling, however, that he was on his way to becoming one of the great legal ballbusters of all time. And under the circumstances I needed to fight fire with fire.

I could have waited until evening and called him at his home, but I was much too frantic to wait. The problem was I had no idea of the name of the law firm he worked for. I had to call a couple of firms just blindly before I could convince a receptionist to look up his name in the city directory—not the regular phone book, but that volume which lists people by their profession—and help me out. Finally, I got the name of the firm.

Then, when I got through, the receptionist in his office tried to give me the brush-off. She said that Paul was in a meeting.

"I don't care what he's in. Tell him it's Richard Schuster calling. I'm certain he'll take the call."

"They're holding the Friday colloquy, Mr. Schuster. I'm sure you under—"

"No, I don't understand. It's an emergency."

"I'm sorry, Mr. Schuster, but—"

"You'll be good and goddam sorry if you don't put him on immediately!"

Click.

I dialed again and apologized to the stupid cunt until we were practically best friends. Then she said that the meeting was breaking up and she'd put me through to Krezney. She put me on "hold." A Muzak tape played

"The Impossible Dream." After a while, a considerably long while, there was a series of electronic clunks on the line.

"Richie?"

"Paul!"

"What's up, buddy?"

"I'm up shit creek without a paddle in a cement canoe."

"Whew . . . you had me worried there for a moment. I thought you were in trouble or something."

"I am, Paul!"

"Calm down, Richie. No need to scream. Count to ten. And don't worry, you can always reverse the charges."

I counted to ten and took a few deep breaths.

"You remember my wife, Sally?"

"Sure. Tall. Sort of ash-blonde. Big tits—"

"Cut it out! This is serious."

"Okay. Sorry. What's the problem?"

"She just threw me out of the house. Our marriage is going down the tubes. She's seeing this lawyer today. I think she's planning to take me to the cleaners, which I don't really care about, because there isn't that much to take anyway, but I don't even know why this is happening. I'm cracking up!"

"You need a lawyer or a psychiatrist?"

"I've already got a fucking psychiatrist. I need a lawyer now!"

"Stop screaming, Richie. Please."

"Okay, okay."

"Let's take this one step at a time—"

"She wants to sock it to me, Paul. She's going straight for the nuts. AND I DON'T KNOW WHY. . . ."

There was a momentary silence at Krezney's end. Then, in a calm, confident voice he replied.

"Look, Rich, the courts don't let them get away with

this kind of crap anymore. Times have changed. Most guys in your situation do not end up getting reamed, and I'll tell you why—"

"Why?"

"I'll tell you why—but first, tell *me*: are there any little ones on the scene since—"

"Little ones? Kids?"

"Exactly."

"No. No kids."

"Okay then. Looks like smooth sailing. A woman like your wife goes into court. Her greaseball counsel tells the court, 'My client demands $300 a week plus the house, plus the car, the furniture, the stereo, the goddam TV set, the *this*, the *that*, the works.' Right?"

"Uh . . . ?"

"The court takes one look at her, sees a perfectly healthy adult individual, and says to himself, 'Who is this slit trying to kid? Let her go out and get a job like anybody else.' You follow me? They fucked themselves good with all this women's lib."

"Great, Paul. Only knowing Sally, she'll show up in a hospital smock and a goddamn wheelchair."

"She better not try it, my friend. The court will see right through it, and she'll pay for her shenanigans."

"Oh, what am I going to do?"

"You're going to stop whining and listen to me, for starters. I'm telling you: there's nothing to worry about. They simply do not allow healthy, childless women to stomp the shit out of their husbands as a moral exercise anymore. At the very worst the court will divide the property in half and tell her to go out and find a job. He might make you pay a little support for a reasonable period while she's out job hunting, let's say ninety days. For three months you pay her rent and buy her a few groceries. After that, she's on her own. And you're out of the woods. Oh, incidentally, what are the grounds?"

"I honestly don't know. Everything just blew up overnight. She told me one night in bed that she never had orgasms. She faked it the whole time we were married. It might sound stupid, but I really freaked out. I found this shrink and started going. She refused to join in the therapy. We stopped talking to each other. It's like my whole life exploded into little fragments without any warning. Anyway, last night I fucked this girl and I think Sally knows it."

"Adultery. Hmmmm . . . She didn't catch you *in flagrante delicto* by any chance, did she?"

"In what . . . ?"

"In the act, Richie, in the act."

"No. No!"

"Well, unless she can produce someone who did, you know, a reliable witness, then *she's* the one who's fucked. She'll have to settle for incompatibility or mental cruelty or some other silly shit."

"This is so depressing I can't believe it."

"Richie, people get divorced every day. It's life."

"It's your bread and butter, you mean."

"Hey, I won't deny it, but—"

"Spare me. What's the next step?"

"Well, first of all, you stop getting fresh with your attorney, who also happens to be your friend."

"I'm sorry, Paul. I really am."

"Okay. I realize you're under a strain. Next, I got to have a look at the Vermont statutes and procedures. Then I got to have a talk with whatever slimy shyster your wife has engaged. Find out his name and leave it with my secretary, would you, Richie?"

"Sure."

"Don't worry. We'll get the message across loud and clear that there is to be no ball-squashing and we'll move this matter though the court quickly, quietly, and without injury to my client, to wit, yourself, ya cluck. Hey, tell me something, Richie: how come you ever married that slit in the first place?"

"I was in love with her."

"I knew it would come to this."

"How did you know?"

"Because she was a wise-ass. Because she didn't know how to give a straight answer. Because she never knew when to stop with the games and back-talk and bullshit."

"That's what you thought back then, huh?"

"That's what I thought, pal."

"She's not that much of a monster. To tell you the truth, I feel kind of sorry for her. She's fucked in the head and she has no desire to correct the problem."

"Save your tears for the judge's chambers."

"Did you ever marry that girl you were living with?"

"Who? Brenda?"

"I think that was her name. The short one with the—"

"Are you kidding me? You think I want to end up like you: up shit creek without a paddle in a cement—"

"Please!"

"Sorry. But seriously, the answer is no. You should see what I'm living with now: she makes Brenda look like a car-hop in a Polish drive-in, which, incidentally, is exactly what she was when I met her: Kinski's Drive-In Red Hots in Lowell, and which, I believe, she has gone back to since the termination of our . . . shall we say . . . arrangement. As for you and me, my friend, we have to make hay while the sun shines."

"I appreciate what you're doing."

"Don't mention it until you see the bill. Listen, I got to go. Some fat slit is coming in here in about five minutes and I got to get ready."

"What's the case?"

"Divorce, shithead."

"Oh. What's she want?"

"Well, figuratively speaking, she wants to drag her husband over a hundred miles of broken light bulbs by his tongue and then drive a loaded gasoline truck up his ass."

"And you're going to help her?"

"Relax, Richie. The lady's got two kids. I'll get back to you in a few days, buddy. Hang in there."

"I will. Bye, Paul."

The rest of the morning I sat in the dim, brown silence of Bob's study wondering over and over and over how and where everything had gone wrong. What with the previous sleepless night, the condition of my brain lent itself to such a trancelike activity. The ashtray filled up as the hours ticked by. Eventually, I noticed that among the books and papers on top of Bob's rather surprisingly orderly desk was a slim volume titled, *A Plague of Locusts*. This collection of Bob's poems, I now realized, was the same book of Bob's that I had encountered and enjoyed so many years ago at Columbia, before I even knew its author. As I scanned its contents, the poems came back to me. Among them was this interesting verse:

DOG SHIT HAIKU

February Thaw
Dog Shit Melts
Wind Blows
Dog Shit Freezes Once Again

It was a little crude, perhaps, but you had to admire the execution. I wasn't sure why he capitalized all the words. Just possibly, I thought, it was a convention of the haiku form—until I remembered that the Japanese don't use the Roman alphabet. Perhaps Bob was attempting to simulate the boldness of oriental pictographs. Did he speak any Japanese himself? I couldn't remember hearing him use any in my presence. As you can see, the poem really stimulated my thinking, at least to the degree that I temporarily forgot about my own personal problems. After a while, I turned the page and read another one:

MAGGOT CIRCUS

Sweet honeybee time
Carolina bee gum rustler
Lumbers through the lumber
Of a Carolina morn
Slumbering animal con
                    Scious
                    Ness
I shoot you fucking
                    INTERLOPER
Sunlight and maggots dance
In the dusty rings
Of your circus eyes
(I's I's I's I's I's I's I's)

While this one might seem at first glance to be a little morbid, it was hard not to admire the energy in the poem, and also his use of Faulknerian Southern themes (i.e., the metaphorical wild beast, the mythic hunt, the curious sing-song quality so evocative of Southern speech).

As for Bob, I guessed that at the time he composed these poems, with their obsessions with death and offal, that he was undergoing some hardship that blackened his art. Possibly, these poems were written during his time in grad school, and I don't have to tell you how grim that experience can be in a young man's life. I figured Bob was doing entirely different work nowadays, though, to tell you the truth, I hadn't seen any of it to this point. Bob never really offered to show me his work-in-progress, and I assumed therefore that he didn't want anybody to see it until it was thoroughly polished and complete.

As I sat there, though, I discovered a yellow legal pad partially tucked beneath a biography of Hart Crane and several volumes of his poetry. There was a poem scrawled on the yellow pad in a tiny, cramped hand, with a lot of scratched out changes and deletions. This is how it went:

PUSSY-PICKING TIME

(Dedicated to the late Jimmie Rodgers)

When it's pussy-picking time in Texas
Nipple-biting time in Tennessee
Asshole-licking time in Alabama
It's gal-humping time for me

Admittedly, the piece is a trifle jejune, but I figured it was just a snatch of doggerel Bob dashed off to amuse himself in an idle moment. I mean, who can say but that Herman Melville or Nathaniel Hawthorne passed their idle hours the same way, tossing off pages of playfully obscene doggerel. (Doesn't Melville, for example, devote a chapter of *Moby Dick* to a description of the whale's incredible dong? And what about the whale's name, after all? Is it outlandish to suppose that the great writer was having a little joke, albeit a bitter one, on his unappreciative audience?)

A series of light, tentative knocks on the door brought me out of my reverie. It turned out to be Annie. She was wondering if I was all right. Though I was ashamed to realize it, I noticed that she wasn't wearing a bra under her rugby shirt. The knit fabric clung closely to the outline of her breasts and you could see the shadow-bump of her nipples as the light caught it. The sight filled me with a kind of unsuppressed horror at my own monstrousness. She entered the room carefully, as if I was a cake in the oven and might collapse at the merest sound. Annie sat down on a brown corduroy love-seat that was half filled with Bob's books.

"What's going on, Rich?" she said eventually, after a long pregnant pause when we both knew the question was inevitable, but during which we examined our fingernails and the ceiling.

"Nothing," I said. "Just had to make some phone calls. I made a bunch of long-distance calls. When you get the bill, just add up all the calls to Boston and I'll give you a check. There'll be a bunch of them."

To tell you the truth, I wasn't really quite sure I could trust Annie. She was, after all, Sally's best friend at Reddington, just as Bob was mine, and I didn't believe that she was about to compromise anything that Sally might have told her in confidence about the deteriorating condition of our marriage.

"Annie, would you mind if I sort of camped out on your sofa for a while, a few days or something?"

"No," she said, "it's all right with me and I'm sure Bob won't mind."

"Great," I said. "Thanks."

We sat there again without speaking for several minutes.

"Would you like a cup of coffee or something, Rich?"

"Gosh, no, Annie, but thanks a lot. Do you happen to know when Bob'll be home?"

"He's got a two o'clock. He'll probably be home after that."

"Great," I said.

Another barely endurable silence. It looked like Annie was just aching to have a meaningful discussion with me—and I don't mean that facetiously either—but it must have been obvious that I was not going to oblige her. So, eventually she took the hint, and with a kind of sigh of frustration said, "Well, I guess you need to be alone for a while, huh, Rich?"

"I really do. Thanks for being understanding, Annie."

She nodded her head, then left the room as carefully as she had come in. When she was gone, I tried to call Dudley—please don't ask me why—but there was no answer. Finally, just to temporarily climb off the merry-go-round of worry and anxiety that was revolving in my head, and to give myself a few minutes of peace, I pulled a huge pictorial history of the Civil War off Bob's bookshelf and immersed myself in it. About an hour and a half later, I could hear Bob's Chevy, with its rotten muffler, coming up the road and pull in the driveway. There was some noise from the other part of the house as Bob came in. I could also hear voices, obviously his and Annie's. Finally, there was a knock on the door. I bounded out of the chair as he came in. He had a can of beer in his hand and pulled the pop-top.

"Boy, am I glad to see you!" I said.

"It's always a pleasure to see you," he replied with a sly grin. "What's going on, buddy? Annie says you've been hiding in here all day long."

"Yes. I guess I have been. Listen, could we get out of here for a little while? Go get a drink somewhere?"

"Sure. The Old Sawmill?"

"No!"

"Okay, relax. I forgot you're not too fond of that place. I know somewheres else we can go. Come on."

We took off in his car. To avoid leaping directly into the presumably boring subject of my disintegrating marriage—until I had a drink in front of me—I mentioned to Bob that I had a chance to read his book, *A Plague of Locusts*, earlier that day.

"Oh," he said with a smile that could not disguise a degree of pain, "that old shit."

"I kind of liked them."

"Apprentice work," he said. "I'm sorry now that I ever published it. Every time I see a copy of the damn thing in some bookstore, I buy the sumbitch and take it home and throw it in the fireplace."

"They were a little morbid, maybe, but so's life. Jesus, so's life. . . ."

"It *can* get grim, I guess. At the time I composed those poems, I was livin' out in the Midwest. My fellowship had just run out—I hadn't written shit the whole damn time I was on it, you understand. Just drinkin' and partyin' and whorin' around the whole time. And then, when I woke up one mornin' and saw that my bank account was overdrawn, well, that's when the party ended and I had to hunker down and get to work—"

"Where was that?"

"Ah, out in Iowa City. Anyway, I was suddenly in very reduced circumstances. Obviously I didn't write the poems for money. But I had to have something to show for my year out there. I finished about a dozen of them, the bulk of the collection, in about three weeks, speedin' my brains out—"

"I know all about it, Bobby," I said.

He suddenly glanced at me with a look of terrible apprehension. It was such a fleeting expression that I wondered if I had interpreted it correctly, and even more, where it came from.

"I was a speed freak in graduate school myself," I explained, and when Bob glanced back in my direction, that fleeting spark of paranoia had been replaced by his customary sly grin.

"Evil shit, idn't it?" he said.

"The worst," I agreed.

"But you got to admit: it sure helps you get the old homework done."

"Indeed it does."

"Anyway," Bob continued, "that's the story of *A Plague of Locusts*. You haven't published yet, have you?"

"Just some academic bullshit. Nothing real."

"Well, take it from me, your early works are a terrible artistic burden that dog you your whole life. They're like idiot children born out of wedlock that you wish you didn't have to acknowledge, but everybody knows they're yours anyway. You'll see what I mean when you've published a few things of your own. It's fuckin' brutal."

I said I imagined it was.

"Only, the stuff I'm workin' on now is a whole lot different," Bob went on. "I'm mining a whole new vein for myself. A lot of it is . . . well, of an erotic nature, so to speak. That stuff in *Locusts*, that was all flies and violence and dead shit. I guess that was my state of mind at the time. But now I'm plugged into a whole new realm of . . . well, like sensuality blended with bits and pieces of pop culture. It's hard to explain."

"You'll have to show me some of it," I said guardedly, remembering that piece of doggerel on his desk and wondering if that was possibly an example of what he was talking about.

"Yeah, I will. It's not really organized yet. I have to do quite a bit of polishing. But I'll be delighted to show it to you after that."

"Great."

We pulled into the dusty parking lot of a roadhouse on Route 7. It was called Ike and Dottie's Tumble Inn. Unlike The Old Sawmill, this establishment didn't pretend to be something other than what it really was: a hick bar for working stiffs. At that hour the parking lot was full of pickup trucks and four-wheel-drive vehicles, and the burly owners were roistering at the bar inside with that kind of cheerful energy unique to men who work

hard with their muscles. The jukebox was blaring country-western music which, though Southern in origin, was
becoming emblematic of the proletariat from sea to
shining sea. Bob ordered a beer and I asked for a Tom
Collins, which caused both Bob and the bartender to look
at me slightly askance.

"When are you gonna quit drinkin' them fruitcake
drinks?" Bob asked. His accent was suddenly as thick as
gumbo.

"You know, for all your education you can be a real
redneck cretin sometimes. Do you think that anybody
who prefers to drink something besides warm beer has
got to be queer?"

"No, I don't automatically make that leap," he said.
"But it's a pretty good indicator, dontcha think?" Clearly,
he was relishing the down-home setting and the opportunity to act like a moron, but then, just as suddenly, he
dropped the accent and the act, and in that less regional
inflection he reserved for important matters, Bob said, "I
hear you might be moving in with us for a few days."

"Sally threw me out of the house. I fucked this girl
last night and didn't come home until this morning."

I suppose I told him so he wouldn't keep treating me
like I was a wimp or something. It wasn't necessary to tell
him, of course. And a moment later, I sort of regretted it
for reasons I did not quite understand at the time. He
merely raised his eyebrows.

"So, when I came home this morning to change, she
packed a couple of suitcases with my stuff and told me to
beat it."

"You're a real heartbreakin' fool," he said.

"That's a very insensitive remark!"

For a second, he seemed stung.

"I guess it was," he eventually agreed.

"This is my life we're talking about."

"I know, and I apologize. Hey, bartender . . ." Bob

drew a little circle with his fingers around our glasses to indicate we were ready for another round. He puffed out his cheeks and sighed demonstrably. "I told you you'd find it distracting around here," he said. "I told you that the first night I met you when we drove around and got high."

"Yes. You did. It's true."

"And you didn't believe me. Didn't *want* to believe me, that is; though deep down, you knew exactly what I was talkin' about."

"Don't give yourself so much credit. That kind of thing can happen anywhere."

Again, Bob looked momentarily stung. And again, the emotion seemed to pass over his face the way a swift-moving cloud throws a momentary shadow over a portion of the landscape and then is gone.

"Anyway, Sally is seeing a lawyer today. We're washed up, I guess, Sally and me."

I started sniffling.

"All I can say is she's got a lot gall throwin' you out like that after all the trouble she put you through with . . . with them orgasms. What are you supposed to do if she won't take care of her husband's needs? It don't even amount to an indiscretion in your case. If you was hungry, you'd go to the refrigerator, right? And if there was no food in it, you'd go out and find yourself some, right?"

"You are obtuse."

"Hey, I'm just tryin' to help. . . ."

"What did Annie say?"

"She said Sally was goin' through some kind of 'changes.' Some kind of vague bullshit like that. It wasn't real fruitful."

"Changes?"

"Yeah."

"She didn't say what kind?"

"I told you, she was real vague."

"I thought you were really going to do some prob-ing."

"Look, I'm not going to act like no private eye for no one."

"Is there some reason why you can't speak English in a place like this?"

"What?"

"Oh, nevermind."

Somebody put a Charlie Rich song on the jukebox about a man whose wife is playing around on him.

"It's a bitch when you lose the one you love," Bob said, partly to himself. "It breaks my heart to think about it. It really does."

The drinks were beginning to catch up on me.

"I'll tell you one thing," I said, also partly to myself, "this boy's not gonna go down without a fight."

"Now you're talking," Bob said without enthusiasm. "Uh, what kind of fight did you have in mind?"

"I don't know yet," I told him. "But I wouldn't want to be around me when the shit hits the fan."

"Don't be thinkin' of nothin' drastic, now."

I looked at him. He seemed to shrink away from me slightly.

"These are drastic times, Bob," I said. "And we must do what the times require."

eight

Losing a loved one is even worse than it's cracked up to be in the country-western ballads. It also propels one in improbable directions. That I sought comfort in the arms (mouth, thighs, etc.) of Alice Dudley Roper, age eighteen, and willful like another, is not so improbable. That I asked her to marry me after five days may better illustrate the extremes toward which I was tending.

It was Wednesday, the first week of November, in her room on Luxury Row. I lay in the bed so redolent of her unique and incomparable fragrance, and gazed through the diamond-shaped fenestration of Dudley's enormous antique window at a cold gray sky. Beneath this window was a college-issue desk littered with expensive artifacts from museum gift shops—objects which Dudley liked to draw and paint (she was an art student). There was a nautilus shell, an enormous African beetle preserved and mounted in a Lucite box, a kite shaped like a bird, a small vase holding peacock and pheasant feathers, a crystal ball.

Dudley was off to my right, preening before the

mirror for her first class of the day. She was wearing a leotard under blue jeans and a loose, white cardigan sweater. She was putting on lip gloss.

For twenty minutes previous, we had argued over my suggestion to go away somewhere for the coming weekend. Dudley did not want to go. She wanted to stay in Reddington and "party" with her friends. In my senile, fuckhead way I tried to spin a sugar-coated picture of our weekend at a country inn—snuggling before the fire, terrific food, long, romantic walks through the woods. But I could easily see that none of this really rang Dudley's bell. When I changed it to an exciting weekend in Boston you could see Dudley actually stop what she was doing for a moment (covering an impertinent zit on her chin with Clearsil) and weigh the pros and cons. But she wrinkled up her nose and said "no" ultimately. Now, she was about to leave and things still had not been settled to my satisfaction.

"What do you say we get married one of these days?" I blurted out.

Was I insane? I think so.

"Are you insane?" Dudley asked, looking at my reflection in the mirror, then turning around to confront me. There was an angry, almost savage glint in her eyes as if she was horribly insulted.

"Insane? Me? No, I'm serious. I mean, maybe not tomorrow or the next day, but some day—"

"Hey, look, it's been real nice and all. You've been fantastic but—"

"I didn't mean it. It was a joke. Ha ha ha ha."

She glared at me suspiciously, then began jamming stuff in her voluminous shoulder bag: pens, pads, Tampax, Kleenex.

"Where are you going?"

"Where do you think? To class."

"But we still haven't settled this, Dudley."

"I'm not going away with you for the weekend, Rich. Period. I want to stick around."

"Do you want to have dinner on Saturday night?"

"I don't know yet."

"Well, what is there to consider?"

"I have to talk to Missy and Bethy and see what they're doing."

"Oh."

Missy and Bethy, you understand, were Dudley's two *best friends*.

"I've got to go now. Would you remember to lock the door when you leave, Rich? You wouldn't believe what a bunch of kleptomaniacs they have around here. Somebody rooked my clock-radio last week, and I just got it too—"

"I don't want to talk about the fucking clock-radio!"

"And I don't want to talk about getting married. Not one teentsy-weentsy bit. Or what I'm going to do this weekend either!"

"Dudley, please. It was a joke. I swear. I don't even know why I said it."

"Some joke."

"I'm losing my marbles. I admit it."

"I've got to go now, Rich."

"Can I call you tonight?"

"I . . . I dunno, Rich."

"I'll call you, and if you feel like it—"

"Okay, fine. You call me. I'm late. I have to go now."

"I'll call you later."

"Fine. Bye."

"Bye."

I listened to her footsteps disappear down the stairs and out of the house. I didn't have a class until one o'clock and I remained in Dudley's bed huddled up in her fragrant sheets as if she too was fading from my life and all that remained of her was that incomparable smell of spice and musk. Eventually my thoughts turned to Sally, and as they did, I began to whimper quietly among the blankets, and as I did, I commenced to perform a rather humdrum sexual exercise with myself right there in Dudley's bed, and when it was over, I burst into tears.

Tell me something: these females I get myself involved with, do I *let* them fuck my head? Is it something I *do?* Do I *create* the conditions that make it possible? Or is it them? Am I attracted to mean women? What's the story? Please God, tell me. . . .

"Of course you create the conditions," Chesmire told me later that afternoon. "You are entirely responsible for your own experience."

"I can't accept that."

"Then you are in big trouble."

I got back to Bob and Annie's house around six o'clock. It was already dark. Neither of their cars were there and neither was at home. I began to feel the strange exhilaration of a kid who is left alone in a house by himself without a babysitter.

There was a bottle of vodka in the freezer where Annie liked to keep it chilled for her favorite libation, vodka and cranberry juice. I made myself a stiff one and retreated to Bob's study. The sofa had been made up into a convertible bed, but was unslept-in, owing to my recent nights at Dudley's. I stretched out on it and kicked off my shoes. Within minutes, I was asleep.

I woke up with a start hours later. The clock on Bob's shelf said 9:30. I felt immediately and horribly lonely. Partly, it was the idea that it was Friday night and I had nowhere to go, while the whole world was out there having a grand time—Sally, Dudley, Missy, Bethy, you name it. Obviously, this was not an exalted sentiment and the smallness of my own peevish little emotions depressed me even more. I began to wonder, with a certain amount of snowballing fear, whether I would ever see Sally again, except in a courtroom. I felt my pulse start to race and my palms sweat. The half-finished drink was on the table next to the sofa. The ice cubes had melted, but I drank it anyway. It was a vile concoction, even worse warm.

I got up and padded across the carpeted room to Bob's desk. The phone seemed to taunt me as I stared at it. I lifted the receiver and held it for several minutes without dialing. Eventually the dial tone turned into a horrible, ear-splitting, ululating noise, like a police siren. The phone flew out of my hands.

"You motherfucker!" I said to the instrument, as if it had acted with deliberate malice.

I went back to the kitchen and made another drink, straight vodka on the rocks this time, then returned to the phone in the study. This time, I placed the call.

Dudley did not answer. Just then it occurred to me that her saying it was all right for me to call did not obligate her to stick around and answer it. Of course, it was past nine-thirty, and even if by some miracle of undeserved loyalty she happened to still be home, then by all rights she would at least be hopping mad, and there would be *that* to deal with. Only, as it turned out, there wasn't even that to deal with. Suddenly, I pictured her in some seamy bar down in the village—not that there were any bistros of this type in Reddington—and I saw her naked to the waist, writhing seductively on a tabletop, while six slobbering pinheads from Dartmouth reached under her whirling skirts. . . .

I let the phone ring and ring and ring while my mind wandered and I finished the vodka. Eventually I hung up and trudged into the kitchen, crying all the way. It was the quality of my crying that really disturbed me, not the crying itself (which I somehow regarded as better than *not* crying). It was just that my crying was taking the form of a sort of self-pitying pule, a very unattractive display even to the one responsible for it. These were certainly not the kind of tears that would move me to console another. They were dismal burlesque tears. They called for a paddle over the head, a swift kick in the pants, or what my father, in his righteous annoyance, used to call a *potch*. I poured another vodka, super-duper stiff. About four fingers (including the ice cubes). Then I did something very bad and very foolish: I called Sally.

"Hello . . . ?"

"Bet you'll never guess who this is," I said cheerfully, though humped with despair inside.

"What do you want, Richard?"

"Richard . . . ?"

"That is your name, isn't it?"

"Oh, God, Sally, don't call me Richard. Please."

Silence at her end.

"Okay," she finally relented. "What is it Rich?"

"I was just wondering what was going on."

"What's going on . . . ?"

"What you were doing."

"Oh. Well, up until just a minute ago I was having a lovely time."

"You alone?"

"Of course I'm alone."

"You want some company?"

"No. Don't come over, Rich."

"Aw, please Sally. I want to see you."

"No, that's not a good idea."

"But Sally, I'm all alone here—"

"Well, I'm alone too, Rich, and I've been having a very pleasant time. Why don't you try and see if you can do the same?"

"I wanna see you."

"But I don't want to see you."

"Aw, come on . . ."

"And if the conversation continues in this vein, I'm not going to talk to you anymore, either."

"Just tell me what I did wrong."

"Oh . . . Rich. Not now."

"Can't you give me a clue?"

"It's too complicated."

"I don't understand anything that's happened. Okay, so you never had an orgasm. I'm sorry for you and I'm sorry for me and I'm sorry I acted like an asshole when you mentioned it. You don't ever have to have one if you don't want. I'll stop having them myself. Then we can both experience—"

"It's not that, Rich."

"What is it then? What? What? What?"

"I told you already: it's complicated."

"I'm a big boy. I can grasp complicated concepts—"

"I'm sure. But I don't want to get into the whole thing now."

"When, then? When? When? When?"

"I don't know."

"It seems to me that sooner or later we're going to have to sit down like a couple of adults and—"

"Sitting down is not going to get us anywhere. Things are under way. Mr. Klein called your pal Krezney this morning—"

"Klein? Who the fuck is this Klein?"

"Edmund Klein is my attorney."

"Oh, *that* Klein."

"You've heard of him?"

"Of course not."

"Oh, it sounded like you had."

"I never heard of any fucking Klein before. Where'd you get him?"

"Does it matter?"

"Of course not. Nothing matters."

"Rich, all I'm trying to get across is that the wheels have been set into motion. We are getting a divorce."

I started to cry again, big choking, lugubrious sobs.

"You probably have no idea how unpleasant it is to listen to someone wailing like that over the phone," Sally remarked.

"I know," I sobbed.

"Isn't there something you can do to take your mind off all this for a while?"

"I don't know."

"What about a nice, warm bath?"

I sobbed even more hysterically. "Okay," I said.

"And don't come over, okay?"

"Okay."

"Promise?"

"I promise."

"Goodbye, Rich."

"Bye, Sally."

She hung up. The tears were getting my neck all wet. I was about to actually get up and take a *nice* warm bath, when I did another strange thing: I called my parents in Oyster Bay. Granted, one turns to Mom and Dad in those hours of darkness. But the fact was, they had no idea we were having any problems and how was I going to explain it to them, when I didn't even understand it myself? I let the phone ring three times, but a sob overwhelmed me and I hastily hung up before anybody could answer it. A few minutes later, the paroxysm over, I dialed again.

"Hello . . . ?" My mom's warm, husky voice (thirty years of scotch and cigarettes).

"Mom . . . ?"

"Richie? Is that you?"

"It's me, Mom, Richie."

"How are you, darling?"

"Fine, Mom, fine—"

"Was that you who called here just a few minutes ago? The phone rang, and just as I was about to answer it—"

"That was me, Mom."

"It was?"

"Yes, Mom. How's—"

"What happened? How come it stopped ringing?"

"I dunno, Mom. This cat jumped on my lap and I had to take care of it."

"Take care of it?"

"Get it off of me."

"I didn't know you had a pussycat."

"I don't."

"Oh. Is it a stray, dear?"

"That's right. It belonged to the people next door."

"Oh . . . ? What happened to them?"

"They . . . they got a divorce and had to move away."

"How sad."

"How's Dad?"

"He's fine, Richie. He's not here now, though, darn it. I know he'd love to talk to you."

"Me too, Mom, me too."

"You would not believe what a . . . what a *jock* he's become lately, darling. He plays squash at the club four nights a week. Eats like a bird. If I didn't know better, I'd think he was trying to impress me. But you know something?"

"What?"

"He looks terrific!"

"That's great to hear."

"When are you and Sally going to come down for a weekend? We miss you so much since you moved."

"I miss you too."

"So, come down for a weekend."

"We will. Soon. I swear."

"Or we could come up. I haven't been to Vermont in twenty years, but there used to be some perfectly lovely inns up there."

"Now's not a good time, Mom. I've got to go now. This cat won't leave me alone."

"Has he had all his shots, Richie?"

"Shots? Sure. Yeah. I guess so."

"Is he fixed?"

"I don't know, Mom. I've got to go."

"Why don't you adopt it?"

"I will. Tomorrow. I promise."

"Then it won't be a stray anymore. It'll have a home and a nice, warm place to sleep when the snow starts to fly. Tell me, are you all right, darling?"

"I'm fine, Mom."

"So nice of you to call."

"Bye, Mom."

"Bye, darling."

The phone kind of slowly slipped out of my hand and bounced off the desk top, snapping me out of one of the trances that were becoming a more frequent feature of my mental life. I placed a couple more calls: one to Krezney at his home in Wellesley and one to Dudley. Neither answered. Wiping my eyes, I lurched into the kitchen for more booze.

It was sometime later, while absent-mindedly examining the bookshelves behind Bob's massive desk, that I came across a curious, typed manuscript. It was sandwiched between two battens of corrugated cardboard held together by criss-crossed rubber bands, and I found it between an *American Heritage* picture history of the American Indian, and another large volume on desperadoes of the Old West. It had been way above eye level, and I had to stand on the chair to withdraw it from its slot. The paper was crinkled, old, erasable bond, stiff with age now and somewhat brittle, like parchment. Imagine my surprise to read the title page:

TARHEEL HERO

a novel by

Robertson Krock

My first impulse was to bind the loose manuscript up again and stick it back in its niche as if I never saw it. But the urge passed quickly, and intense feelings of curiosity and temptation took its place. I lit a cigarette and cleared a portion of the desk to accommodate the bulky document.

The story concerned the peregrinations and adventures of a North Carolinian stud named Tee Dancer in the world of stock-car racing during the late 1950s. Tee is the son of a dirt-farmer from a tiny village near the seacoast. At sixteen, he goes to work in a pulp mill, but after a fistfight with a brutal foreman, he splits for Florida to take up his dream career as a stock-car racer. About every fifty miles between his home and Daytona, Tee screws a different woman. None of them satisfy his incredible lust.

Down in Daytona, Tee wangles a job on the pit crew of a racing team, but within a remarkably short time, he gets a chance to drive in his first race. Meanwhile, he gets mixed up with the daughter of the biggest car dealer in South Florida. This car dealer, a Big Daddy type straight out of Tennessee Williams, has risen out of the depths of white trash society to become one of the richest men in the state. But he's tremendously sensitive about his origins and the image he presents to the public. So, when he finds out his daughter, Barbara, is hanging out with this stud of a Carolina cracker, Big Daddy sends one of his goons down to the pit at three in the morning to monkey around with Tee's modified Chevy. The next day, in the middle of a qualifying heat, Tee's car sucks a valve and he puts it into the wall.

Miraculously, though, Tee escapes mortal injury. In the meantime Barbara overhears a conversation between her Daddy and a henchman, and learns that he is responsible for Tee's near-fatal "accident." She loses all respect for her father and defies him by leaving home to help nurse Tee back to health again. Only now, Tee's got one thing on his mind: revenge. He makes an elaborate plan to drive his car right into Big Daddy's grandstand box during the running of the Daytona 500 and kill the bastard. Not that Tee wants to commit suicide, you understand—he plans to bail out of the vehicle just before it hits.

The day of the big race arrives. Somehow, Barbara has gotten wind of Tee's scheme to assassinate her father from this guy on the pit crew, a comic-relief Mickey Rooney-type named Tiny. Just before the race, Barbara finds Tee and pleads with him not to kill her daddy, lest he (Tee) turn into the same sort of heartless scumbag as her father. She tells him he was cut out to be a poet, not a stock-car racer, and that the two of them should get out of Florida somehow and go someplace where Tee can "be somebody."

The race scene is the climax, naturally. For the first ninety-nine laps, Tee struggles with his various alternatives. He knows also that deep down he's really the sensitive poetic type, but he also feels that he's "somebody" in the world of stock-car racing and can hardly stand to give up the adulation of his redneck fans. Finally, though, poetry wins out. He decides to spare Big Daddy's life. He wins the race, but it is to be his last.

In the epilogue, Tee and Barbara go north to "the land of learning," as she calls it, where they jointly enroll in a "big university." They live happily ever after. What a crock of shit.

About halfway through, I recognized the story as the basis for a 1964 movie *Wheels on Fire*, with Tab Hunter and Ann-Margret, which, oddly enough, had played on the late show not more than a month earlier. Only in the movie, the Barbara character was the daughter of a rich ex-Nazi industrialist who sponsors a "Formula One" team. And the racing settings were switched from Florida to the Grand Prix tracks of Europe. Tee Dancer, though, remained the character's moniker, and he was still basically the same violent, Carolinian jerk-off. The type-script was only 170 pages long, hardly publishable length. No wonder Mac had freaked out when the "famous personage" presented him with this skimpy package of goods. And the "famous personage," himself . . . ?

I couldn't believe what a purblind asshole I was for not realizing it sooner, for not knowing way back on the July evening over a year ago when he (almost compulsively, I now thought) briefed me on the details of Mac's crimes, that he himself was the logical accessory. I supposed that the term "famous personage" had thrown me off completely. I hadn't taken it for the combination of guilty irony and megalomania that it truly stood for.

Oddly enough, though, Roberston Krock's stock as a poet was rising steadily. *A Plague of Locusts* had won him the Hulot Prize for 1968. He had won a Guggenheim the following year and traveled to the Far East. Magazines like the *Atlantic* and *The New Yorker* were hospitable to him and printed his verses. And now, here he was, secure and salaried at Reddington, a wild Carolina boar in a glade of clover. Well, I sighed and thought to myself, at the time he no doubt desperately needed the money.

I reassembled the manuscript and put on the rubber bands. Among the books and papers I had shoved aside to clear a space was that legal pad with its fragment of doggerel: "Pussy-Picking Time." After returning *Tarheel Hero* to its niche on the shelf, I stared at that snatch of doggerel for a long time.

". . . I'm mining a whole new vein for myself . . ." he had said, *". . . of an erotic nature. . . ."*

I wondered now: was this the work of man troubled in his art?

It was after midnight. I was hardly even high anymore, having read *Tarheel Hero* in a single straight sitting. I went into the kitchen and poured myself a fresh drink. The house was incredibly still. Never before had I been so aware of the awesome quiet of the country. Always, before, there had been someone else in the house, someone moving, listening to music, cooking, bathing, at least breathing. At first, I was merely fascinated by the quiet, then, all of a sudden, terribly frightened. I rushed back into Bob's office and picked up the phone, nervously dialing the number.

"Hello, Dudley?"

"Rich. . . ?"

"Yes. It's me. Are you awake?"

There was a groan.

"Okay, I'm sorry," I said. "Stupid question."

"It's all right."

"You doing anything?"

"Getting ready to go to sleep."

"I see. I called you a couple of times."

"Did you?"

"I said I would."

"Yes. I guess you did."

"You were out, though, I guess."

"We went down to the village for a while."

"You and your friends?"

"That's right. I'm really wasted."

"I've been reading all night."

"Really? Great."

"Yeah, just sitting around by myself."

"Did you have a good time?"

"Smashing."

"Well, that's good."

"Would you like it if I dropped over for a little while, Dudley. I'd like to see you."

"I don't think so, Rich. I'm so wasted."

"How about just a little while?"

"I'd love to, Rich, but—"

"If you'd love to, then I'll come down."

"Not tonight. Please."

"Look, goddammit, I really want to see you. I'm all alone here."

"You don't have to get angry."

"I'm sorry. Listen, I'll just come down for a little while. A half an hour or something. That's all."

"Rich, I'm too wasted to . . . to do that tonight. So it would be totally pointless, if that's what you have in mind. Don't you see?"

"Who said I had *that* in mind. I just want to be with somebody."

"I want to go to sleep. Can't you just go to sleep too, where you are? I'm sure you'll feel better in the morning."

"But I want to feel good now."

"Rich, you're being so childish."

"I know. I'm ashamed of myself. But that's how I feel."

For a long time neither of us said anything, though I could hear her breathing into the phone. I hoped she was changing her mind.

"What do you say, Dudley?"

"I'm sorry, but the answer is still no."

Another pause. I was tempted to blow my stack but somehow managed to divert the impulse to a more constructive direction.

"All right," I told her. "You win. But let's at least have dinner tomorrow night."

"Okay," she said.

I was glad that I had managed to control myself after all. At least I wouldn't have to be alone the following night.

"Did you have a good time down in the village?" I asked her.

"Yes! I danced my ass off."

"That sounds like fun I guess."

"It was great. Can I hang up now, Rich."

"Uh . . . sure."

"Okay, I'll see you tomorrow night, then."

"Uh . . . that's right."

"Goodnight baby," she said in a voice full of sex and sleep.

"Goodnight, Dudley."

Why was I disturbed to hear that she had had a "good time?" Did I object to her teenager's idea of what it comprised, e.g. dancing her ass off? The truth is, though I couldn't admit it to myself, the whole conversation pissed me off tremendously. When you really get down to it, I thought, an eighteen-year-old was jerking me around, and I didn't like it.

On the other hand, why add age-chauvinism to my growing list of personality deformities. If she was tired, she was tired. She had that right no matter what age she was. Obviously, I was over-reacting. In any case, as long as she was safe and happy in her trundle bed, then there was no reason, certainly no *need* to freak out over it. Meanwhile, the open convertible sofa, all made up with fresh sheets and warm blankets, beckoned me seductively across the room. I resigned myself to it, selecting a particularly dull volume of Henry James from the book-shelf to help the process along. My head felt like it was filled with Jello from all the drinking. I read for a couple of minutes, then reached up to the nearby table for the light.

I must have been in a near-coma because I never heard the car pull in, never heard her enter the house or creep into the room, didn't feel her slip under the covers, didn't know she was there until slowly, dreamily, I became aware of the warmth radiating off of another's body. Of course, having been married for nearly six years, I was used to the sensation. What nudged me to consciousness was the smell. It was not Sally's characteristic fragrance of sweet berries, nor even Dudley's perfume of spice and musk. Suddenly, I was mortified.

"Annie . . . ?"

"Yes."

"Oh no. . . ."

"Hush—"

"This is a very bad idea, Annie."

I reached for the light and switched it on. For several moments I was stone blind. Then I saw her huddling under the blankets. She had them pulled over her head.

"Please turn it off," she said.

"No, Annie. You've got to get out of here."

She threw back the blankets, reached behind her back, and turned off the lamp. As she did, a little gust of her own sweet smell wafted my way. I also noticed how sleek her body was. Her breasts were the wide, tear-shaped type of a woman in her thirties, attractive because they suggested maturity. Even from a distance of several inches I could feel the radiant heat of her body, and it disturbed me wildly.

"Annie, please! This is crazy. Bob'll kill—"

"Bob's not here," she said in a tone of voice that could not conceal either her anger or determination.

"Not here . . . ? What time is it?"

"After three. In the morning."

"W-where is he . . . ?"

"I don't know," she said, as if it was something a good deal more than a matter of fact. Then, she shrank back into the covers. "My guess is he's with one of his students."

"I'm . . . I'm sorry, Annie."

"Didn't you know that about my husband?"

"No," I said sadly and dishonestly.

"Well, that's where he is."

"Is this revenge? Annie?"

"I don't know," she said with a crick in her voice. Then she reached over and pulled herself toward me, into the pocket formed by my boomerang-like position. But it was not a gesture of desire on her part, or even affection necessarily. It was more like the response of a cold child seeking warmth. To my further horror, I felt myself getting an erection. A moment later, I leaped out of bed and grabbed my pants.

"Please, Rich. Don't go."

"I have to Annie. I'm sorry. Things are getting so weird I can't handle any of it anymore. You're pretty and nice and sweet and smart and I like you very much, but I can't handle this. I have to go."

I was shaking like one of those little plastic windup toys that you set on a table and watch dance madly around till they fall off the edge and crash. I didn't bother tying my shoes, and on the way out of the house, one of the laces caught in the front door, sending me sprawling over Bob's cement portico onto the hard, frozen grass. As I started the Volvo, I noticed a light go on in an upstairs room, Bob and Annie's bedroom.

Please, I thought to myself, please nobody hurt themselves.

The logical place of refuge: Dudley's, of course. I knew it before I passed Mac's house down the road from Bob's. The spotlights were on and it never looked more like a piece of sheer magnificent sculpture than now against the bare black branches of the autumn woods.

The front door to Dudley's dorm—an elegant mansion behind the old Redding Hotel—was locked. I prowled up and down the long front porch looking for an alternative means of entry. Just up the street, the battle monument was visible in the center of the old village commons. The obelisk was bathed in moonlight, proud, erect and fundamentally absurd. I tried the windows and found one that was ajar. Moments later, I was within the building: a criminal.

The once-again antique plumbing (the building was restored, remember, back in the twenties) coughed musically throughout the house. Otherwise, all was quiet. The room I was in was kind of a living room, filled with the hardy, indestructible Danish-modern furniture one associates with institutional housing. A TV set in one corner was surrounded by Naugahyde-covered easy chairs. Empty soda cans and snack food effluvia littered the carpet. I imagined all the young women in their warm rooms above, arrayed in the various attitudes of sleep, in various degrees of undress. The image sent a shudder down my spine, and I wondered if maybe I ought to leave that instant. Jungle noises—that now-familiar demi-hallucination—began welling in a remote corner of my brain. I proceeded upstairs.

I stood outside her door for a minute or more, wondering whether to knock, or if that would make too much noise. I tried the knob. The door was not locked. I opened it. A struggle of some kind was in progress on the bed. Startled, I momentarily ducked back out into the hall, then threw the door open violently and switched on the light. Poised on his haunches above Dudley, his handsome middle-aged face distorted into a fleering mask of lust, his tumescent organ hanging beneath his buttocks like some heinous and distinctly primordial life form— say, a glistening sea-slug—was Mac MacWhorter. Dudley's knees dangled absurdly in the air for a moment, then fell as she reached desperately to cover herself with a sheet.

"Oh shit . . . ."

"I *told* you not to come here!" Dudley cried in a strangled voice. Mac, meanwhile, had more or less vaulted over her and was himself scrambling for cover.

"I thought you were alone!" I said, not as an accusation, but as if it explained my sudden appearance. I found myself shrinking backward until my rear end bumped up against Dudley's desk with its clutter of natural history artifacts. Once there, I cleared a little space on the corner and sat down on it so as to pause and absorb my feeling of shock.

"Well, *obviously* she's not alone, Schuster," Mac said with an effort at diplomacy. "Now that you've had a good look, would you be kind enough to leave?"

"Oh, I can't leave," I said, mainly to myself, and not entirely clear even in my own mind what I meant by it, or what conditions would have to obtain before it was possible to leave.

"But you must leave, and leave now," Mac replied, still calm and reasonable—the tone of voice of one who was accustomed to command. "You must leave at once," he added.

"I must . . . ?"

"Yes, Schuster. This very minute. Without delay."

"But . . . but you're here."

"That's true. And so are you, for the moment. And you must leave."

"You said you were alone," I looked now at Dudley.

"I didn't say that," she replied timidly.

"Perhaps she meant to spare your feelings, Shu—"

"I'm not talking to you, Mac. I'm talking to Dudley."

"Goodbye, Schuster."

"I thought you said you were—"

"Get out, Schuster!"

"Interrupt again, Mac, and you'll regret it."

"Oh! Big Man."

"I'm not kidding."

Mac threw off his part of the sheet and made as if he was going to come after me. I wheeled around and searched the surface of the desk. There was a pair of those heavy pliers Dudley used for stretching canvases and I seized the formidable tool.

"Stay where you are, Mac."

"Are you nuts?"

"No, I'm pissed off."

"You're insane, Schuster—look, I'm not going to be threatened."

He made another move and I hoisted the pliers violently overhead to show that I meant business. He shrank back onto the bed.

"If you're making this big scene for my benefit, you can stop now," Dudley said wearily, her voice no longer timid but full of disgust. "It's not going to help anything."

"Why did you lie to me?"

"I don't know who you think I am, Rich. But I'm not your wife. I'm not married to you, even though you want me to be—"

"He asked you to marry him?" Mac turned to his companion in bed.

"That's none of your goddam business, Mac!"

Mac began laughing hysterically.

"I admit it, it was stupid, Dudley. It was a mistake. I don't know what made me say it."

"Rich, you've got to leave."

"I know, but—"

"No, Rich, arguing right now isn't going to solve anything."

"You'd rather stay with this . . . this senile pansy-ass?"

"Name-calling is not going to help, either. Now, put down those pliers and go over to the door and open it and walk downstairs and go home and we'll talk about it tomorrow."

"Promise?"

"Yes."

For some reason, I followed her instructions, though I hesitated at the door, where the impulse to knock Mac's teeth down his throat continued to dog me. Then I remembered Sally's admonition about the State Penitentiary. I pictured myself teaching *Fun with Dick and Jane* to my fellow prisoners.

"What— will you call me? Or should I call you?" I asked without turning back to look at her.

"Whatever," Dudley said. "But go for now."

"Okay."

I turned the knob and shuffled out. There were footfalls immediately from within, and the heavy metallic click as Dudley threw the deadbolt.

Out in the hallway, half a dozen girls stood in their pastel-colored bathrobes. Their faces were full of apprehension.

"It's all right, ladies," I said. "Just a little mix-up. Go back to your rooms now. It's all right."

They followed me downstairs though, keeping their distance and whispering behind me. As I stepped out onto the porch, I heard them re-bolt the front door too. Then, they all ran around the first floor checking the locks on the windows and securing them wherever necessary. Moonlight still blazed off the obelisk. The sight of it suddenly evoked musket fire and the brassy sound of bugles.

I got into the Volvo and fired it up. I didn't have any particular destination in mind, though I suppose I had a desire to get a drink because I found myself leaving the campus and barreling down the mountainside into the valley and the village of Reddington.

Once down there, though, a cursory circuit of the quiet streets showed that none of the town's four or five bars was still open. A clock in the bank's neo-classical pediment said 4:15.

I sat in front of the stoplight at the main intersection

and watched it change a dozen times or more while I tried to figure out what to do, where to go. There was no other traffic whatsoever. It occurred to me to check into a motel, but I suddenly realized that I had forgotten my wallet, left it in Bob's study in my haste to escape his house earlier. Returning there at this point seemed utterly out of the question. There seemed to be only one practical alternative left: to go home. I could slip inside without waking Sally and grab a few hours sleep on the sofa in the living room. If she found me there in the morning, it would just be tough-shit. I'd apologize and leave. No more scenes. I didn't think I could take any more scenes. We tend to underestimate ourselves that way.

On my way back up the mountain, it started to snow. It was the first snowfall of the season. The flakes were the big wet sticky kind which turn to slush as soon as they hit the windshield. The faster I drove, the faster the flakes rushed at me, and when I switched from the low-beams to my brights, the effect was dazzling. For a few moments I pretended I was a World War II bomber pilot deep in enemy territory on a night mission and that the snow-flakes were a shitstorm of anti-aircraft flak. It was hyp-notic. I even dodged the car back and forth across the road, delighting in minor fishtails and skids.

Suddenly, though, the snowflakes stopped being anti-aircraft fire and I started to think that faces were rushing at me: Sally, Dudley, Annie, Bob, Mac, Paul Krezney, old faces from Cambridge, from Columbia, from high school, summer camp, even a few characters who looked like the sinister Hugo of yore. I grew frightened. My heart started beating like crazy and my palms broke out in sweat. I slammed on the brakes and the car did a 360-degree turn, miraculously staying on the road and coming to a stop with the gentlest of bumps—hardly even a collision—against the bronze and wood sign that said REDDINGTON COLLEGE. The car had hit the sign in the left quarter panel. I turned off the engine, clawed at the door handle and lurched outside. To tell you the truth, I thought I was having a heart attack, though it was nothing of the kind. I was just temporarily overwhelmed with anxiety, and squatted in the gravel next to the car taking deep lungfuls of cold air. After a few minutes, I felt better. I stood up and walked around the car to check the damage. There was just a little ding where the corner of the enormous sign stopped the car. The snow was sticking in my hair and eyelashes and I began to notice how cold it was out. A moment later, I was back in the car and on the road again.

Snow now swirled around the lonely obelisk. The heart of the campus seemed like a village of the dead. Here and there an electric light burned fuzzily over the empty streets. I pulled around the commons, swerved past the gymnasium, and took the road which led to several of the dorm clusters and, ultimately, our old farmhouse.

When I got to the birchwood between the Granary and the old house, I slowed the car down to a crawl and turned off the headlights so as not to wake Sally. Even with the snow, there was a kind of incandescent swell of light all around to see by. As I inched up the driveway, I encountered an eerily familiar shape. My heart plunged. Parked in the driveway was an old, white Chevrolet.

This can't be, I thought at first. Then, my incomprehension—falling away like the skin of a creature in molt, and suddenly alive to a whole dimension of things previously impossible, and wanting now to really go forth and see where they might lead . . .

We change. We commit acts seemingly only feasible for strangers and we wonder, who are these strangers? These strangers are . . . me! As I stepped from the car, all fear seemed to flutter away like crows evacuating the branches of a dead tree at a sound unheard by human ears. There was a sense in me as of someone "on the loose."

I marched into the house taking no pains to be stealthy.

"Krock, you two-faced cornholing motherfucker!"

No answer. Not that I expected one. Nor did I wait for one. It was more a matter of merely announcing my presence than a call to combat. *C'est moi!*

Suddenly I felt a compelling—an overwhelming— desire to listen to music, and rooted through the record collection in the living room until I found exactly what the moment required—a perfectly horrible Iron Butterfly album from the long-gone epoch of peace and love. Humming busily to myself, I readied the equipment and turned the volume knob to its upper limit. The moment the cartridge alighted on the vinyl, you could feel the speakers quiver and strain. When the music commenced, the speakers immediately blew. I didn't care. It sounded even better that way, keener and more hateful. Then I turned on the television. There were no programs on at that hour, but the NBC affiliate in North Adams, Mass., was putting out a terrific test-pattern accompanied by a splendid high-pitched electronic wail. I turned it up as high as possible and headed into the kitchen.

Above the sink, on the windowsill, was the smaller KLH FM receiver that Sally liked to listen to while she prepared her organic delicacies. I found a station playing soul music and turned it up to top volume. Harold Melvin and the Blue Notes vied hopelessly with the acid generation for supremacy of the airwaves. It was delightful. To further enhance the effect I was trying to create, I switched on the blender, the dishwasher, and the juicer. Then, suddenly caught up in a new and wholly different inspiration, I slipped hastily out the back door and loped across the lawn to the car.

Five minutes later, I pulled into the driveway of Bob's

house. The door was unlocked and I went inside. Annie blinked as I turned on the light at her bedside.

"Rich . . . ?" she said, sounding neither surprised nor upset, but merely confirming the fact of her wakefullness.

"Yes," I said. "It's me."

She held her hand above her eyes, shielding them from the light.

"What are you doing?"

"Visiting," I said.

"Oh. Where have you been?"

"Out."

"Where?"

"Nowhere."

"Oh . . . ."

I undid my belt and unzipped my fly.

"Have you been drinking?"

"No, darn it, I haven't," I replied, snapping my fingers. "Thanks for reminding me. I've been wanting a drink for a while now."

Then, with my pants dangling around my knees, I shimmied down to the kitchen, yanked the bottle of vodka from the freezer, and glugged down what probably would have comprised several generous drinks at once.

When I returned to the bedroom, Annie was propped against the wicker headboard, the blankets smoothed out carefully over her body, and a cigarette held somewhat to the right of, and about at the same level of, her ear. She nibbled her lower lip as if she was growing suspicious of the precise nature of the program I had in mind. I stood there for a while, pants half down and vodka bottle dangling from my hand. Annie forced a smile. I reached down and yanked the sheets and blankets off both her and the bed itself. The smile quickly vanished. Her body jerked spasmodically for an instant but she did not try to cover her nakedness or move or leave the bed. I relieved her of her cigarette and smashed it out in the ashtray atop her clock-radio.

"What on Earth has gotten into you, Rich?"

"Nothing. I just thought we'd pick things up where we left off a while ago."

"It's five in the morning."

"That's right. Care for a drink?"

She shook her head.

"You have a very nice body, Annie."

"Thank you. I'm not sure I like this, Rich."

"You'll like it. I promise."

"I don't like the way you're acting."

"I offered you a drink, didn't I? That was good manners, wasn't it?"

Annie sighed. The corners of her mouth quavered as in the prelude to tears. Meanwhile, I pulled my shorts down and let them dangle at my ankles along with the pants.

"You're going to rape me now, aren't you?" Annie said.

"Of course I'm going to rape you."

"You could have had it before without even asking."

"I know. I suppose it's not really rape, though, technically speaking, under the circumstances."

She made a face. It expressed something that was not quite pity or despair but a sentiment roughly between the two.

"Come on, Annie. Spread 'em."

She slid down the headboard and spread her legs as I instructed.

"I'm not wet," she said sadly. "You're acting so weird that I'm not even wet." Her eyes had grown red and the corners were now moist with teardrops.

"That's okay," I said, easing myself on top of her and forcing my way between the soft, pliant, but not es-

pecially slippery tissues. At length, and with some difficulty, I managed to gain entry. "That's okay, Annie.
That's okay. That's okay, that's okay, that's okay, that's
. . . ugh . . . okay, that's . . . ughah . . . okayugh, tha
. . . tha . . . tha . . . thathathathathathaaaaaaaaaaaaaaaaa
. . ."

It was over pretty quickly. I lay there for a minute or
so on top of her, panting. The vodka bottle was still in my
left hand. The stuff I had glugged down in the kitchen
was already working. Slowly, I dragged myself off of
Annie and allowed myself to roll off the edge of the bed. I
landed on the carpet with a thud, took another long
drink, and struggled to pull my pants back on. My thighs
were all sticky and it did not feel good under the pants, so
I went into the bathroom and washed.

When I returned to the bedroom, Annie was smoking
again. And crying, visibly, though quietly.

"I'm sorry, Annie. That's all there is tonight. I have
to go now."

She closed her eyes and turned her head away.

"Don't cry, Annie. Please."

"I'm afraid for you," she said with a sob. "Don't go."

"I have to, Annie," I said, as if it was only reasonable. "I have to and I must leave at once."

She flung herself onto her stomach, her back humped
with sobs. The cigarette was still burning in her out-
stretched hand, and I removed it.

Down in Bob's study, I yanked the manuscript of
Tarheel Hero off the shelf and stuffed it in my jacket. My
wallet was lying on the table next to the open convertible
sofa. When I got to the front door, Annie was blocking it.
She pleaded with me once more to not leave the house,
but I moved her out of the way as gently as possible and
marched out to the car. I jammed the manuscript under
the seat and turned over the engine. As I pulled away, I

could see her standing in the doorway, naked and exposed to the freezing air.

The Green Mountains were visible to the east, silhouetted now against the pink band of sky that precedes a cold country dawn. The snow had stopped and a scant inch or so covered the ground. My car laid the first tracks through it along the pristine road. A child's red-and-yellow plastic tricycle sat in the center of Mac's driveway. I felt it crunch beneath my front wheels as I brought the Volvo to a stop.

The doorbell played the first two bars of the song "Hernando's Hideaway" from a Broadway musical of the fifties. How like that asshole, I thought. I leaned on the button so that the melody persistently repeated itself. At last, there was thumping within, as of someone coming down the stairs. A blurred figure peered out at me through the side panels of corrugated glass, apparently unable to make out my identity.

"Mac . . . ?" It was Cleo's voice.

"No, it's me, Richard Schuster."

"Who?"

"Richard Schuster, the new guy in the English department. Remember?"

"Oh . . . yes, Richard. Just a second."

I heard her unlock the door and also take a chain off. She was wearing a black silk kimono with snorting dragons embroidered on it. Even rudely awakened, she was an undeniably handsome woman. I stepped inside, blew on my hands, and rubbed them together briskly.

"Cold as hell out there," I observed.

"I thought you were Mac," Cleo said, trying to conceal her embarrassment.

"Oh, golly," I said. "You mean Mac's not here, then?"

Cleo tried to force a smile, but it came out more like a

cracked little frown. She looked at me and then down at the carpet.

"Well, gosh, I have an idea. Let's you and I wait for him."

She looked back at me sharply, a puzzled tremor at the corners of her mouth.

"Yes," I explained cheerfully, "let's you and I wait for Mac. And let's have a fire while we wait, huh? That would be nice, wouldn't it? On such a chilly morning here in the country, a nice fire?"

Before she could agree, I marched into the living room with its cathedral ceiling and its ultra-modern, chrome-and-leather furniture. There was a box of kindling and a stack of old newspapers beside the huge, fieldstone fireplace, as well as half a dozen birch logs. I got down and crumpled several sheets of paper into balls, shoved them beneath the grate, and built a teepee of kindling over it. One match got the clever arrangement going and I warmed my palms before the flames.

"Isn't this great?" I said.

Cleo did not reply, but when I looked over at her, she nodded her head vigorously in agreement. Her arms were crossed, not defiantly, but as though she were holding onto herself for protection.

"Do you know what would also be real nice?" I said. "Some marshmallows. Do you have any marshmallows, Cleo?"

She stared at me blankly for a moment, her mouth slightly agape.

"No?" I asked.

"I'm . . . I'm not sure," she finally said. "I'll go in the kitchen and look."

"Great. You do that. I'll get this fire going real good while you get the marshmallows."

When she was gone, I went over to the other wall and flung open the polished oak doors of the cabinet which held Mac's videotape and playback equipment. Another cabinet door opened to reveal shelves of neatly stacked audio and video cassettes in various boxes, all indexed and each with a typed name on its spine: Allen Ginsberg, James Dickey, W.S. Merwin, Karl Shapiro, Galway Kinnell, Robert Bly, Creeley, Corso, Oppenheimer, O'Hara, et cetera, et cetera, et cetera. Beneath this fabulous archive of taped interviews with great poets of mid–twentieth-century America was a well-stocked bar. I seized a bottle of Hennessey Cognac and pulled the cork with my teeth. Then I thought of something rather urgent and dashed into the kitchen. As I suspected, Cleo was dialing the phone.

I took the receiver out of her hand and pressed down the little lever on the wall box.

"You're not doing your job," I told her. "Your job is to get marshmallows, not to make phone calls." And for emphasis, I ripped the receiver cord out of the housing. "Now, let's find those marshmallows."

Cleo went to a cabinet above a butcher-block counter, rummaged around for a minute, and withdrew a bag of pastel-colored marshmallows: pink ones, green ones, yellow ones.

"What a find!" I said.

Cleo, I noticed just then, was crying. I put my hand on her shoulder. She shrank away slightly at my touch, but didn't try to run or leave the room.

"Look," I said to her quietly and reassuringly, "I realize that you're frightened, but I'm not going to do anything to hurt you. Believe me. Do you believe me?"

She didn't say. She merely gazed into the tile floor.

"You think I'm acting crazy, don't you?"

She shuddered.

"You can be honest."

She looked up at me finally and with big, sad, watery eyes, she nodded her head.

"It's true," I admitted. "I'm in the process of running amok. There's no question about it. But don't think I lack insight. It may sound even crazier to you, but I know exactly what I'm doing. Now, come on, let's go into the other room and roast a few of these marshmallows and wait for Mac to come home, okay?"

Cleo nodded again.

"That's my girl," I said, and gave her an affectionate squeeze, then steered her back into the living room. She sat down on the chrome-and-leather sofa in front of the fireplace. I took a slug of brandy, put the bottle down, and began transporting boxes of tapes from the cabinet to the floor next to the hearth. When I discovered the box marked Robertson Krock, 1971, I couldn't help but let out a little yelp of delight.

"Do you know how to work this equipment, Cleo?"

"Yes."

"Would you mind putting this tape on for me?"

She hesitated for a moment, sighed dejectedly, then got up and put the tape on. She switched on the TV and after several moments of colored confetti-like static, the picture resolved. The silhouettes of two figures could be seen against a backlighted studio set. It was not a snazzy production, but the tape was of decent quality. Next, the graphics began to roll. A voice-over announced the program: "Another in the continuing series of the Reddington Poet's Forum . . . today, a dialogue with Robertson Krock . . ."

The lights came up on Bob and Mac as the camera moved in. They both looked younger, especially Mac, whose hair was noticeably darker. Krock, for his part, evidently affected more of a hippie-like appearance back in those days. He wore jeans and a kind of blowsy Lord Byron-type of white cottony shirt, and his hair was longer, a thick black mop that fell over his ears.

"It's nice to have you here with us today," Mac

began. Evidently, the interview had taken place a year or two before Bob joined the faculty. Mac held up a copy of *A Plague of Locusts.*

Cleo had returned to her seat on the sofa. I helped myself to some more brandy, then turned my attention to the fireplace. The blaze was going great guns by this time and I threw a couple of logs on top of the roaring kindling. It took about a dozen trips from the shelves to the fireplace before I had all the tapes conveniently stacked. Cleo shaded her eyes with a hand as if she was afraid to see what would happen next and the corners of her mouth twitched. I put the first two tapes in the fire to see how well they would burn. James Wright and Richard Wilbur went up on a column of dense black smoke. I threw in some more kindling and then four more tapes and opened the marshmallows. Using the brass fire poker in lieu of something better, I stuck a pink marshmallow on the end, let it catch, and extinguished the pretty blue flame when the marshmallow was nice and shiny-black. I offered the delicacy first to Cleo, but she declined, so I ate it.

" . . . your poems here in *Locusts,*" Mac said on the screen in reference to Bob's book, "are full of images of wild, lumbering beasts, in this case a bear. . . ."

I fired up another marshmallow and watched the tape. As the interview proceeded, Bob seemed to slump deeper and deeper into his chair, his answers to Mac's questions grew increasingly terse. His eyes, also, began to flash paranoically.

"Look at him ham it up!" I remarked to Cleo, meanwhile chucking a few more tapes onto the fire. (Gary Snyder, Leroi Jones).

"Those things are my husband's whole life!" she suddenly blurted out and started sobbing.

Frankly, the outburst caught me rather off guard. To that point, I honestly hadn't considered her feelings about the destruction I was perpetrating. If anything, perhaps, I had naively assumed that she shared a kind of secret glee over the desecration. Clearly, it was not that simple.

"His whole life's work!" Cleo sobbed.

"Actually," I told her, sticking another marshmallow on the poker, "your husband's a more well-rounded person than you might think. Take his sex life, for instance. Do you know where he is now?"

"Yes," she said emphatically.

"Oh. . . ."

Cleo stuck a knuckle in her mouth and squeezed her eyes closed. As she did, tears coursed down her cheeks.

"I don't mean to be insensitive about it—"

She sobbed wildly.

"—but are you taking care of your needs?"

Her eyes opened suddenly, the glint of terror in them.

"I thought you said you weren't going to . . . to hurt me," she said feebly.

"Oh no. Look, I'm not going to rape you or anything, for Godsake, Cleo. I just thought, well, heck, we've got a fire going and all, and marshmallows, and, well, frankly you're a damn good-looking woman. As far as I can see, Mac must be crazy to—"

"You're the one who's crazy! And you better not try it!"

"Relax. I just thought—"

"And you're going to be sorry that you ever set foot in this house."

"I don't know. I'm having a pretty good time. Marshmallow?"

"You're going to regret this."

"Jeez, you don't have to get all huffy about it—"

"Just wait until the authorities get through with you."

"Get through with what?"

"Reaming your butt!"

"Nobody's going to ream my butt."

"We'll see about that."

"Okay," I said, "if that's how you want to be—"

I heard a car pull into the driveway outside. Two doors slammed. I reached over and dropped an armload of tapes onto the fire.

"Sounds like the lord of the manor is home."

I stuck another marshmallow on the poker, lit it up and leaned against the coffee table so I could see the foyer. There was a jingle of keys, then the door opened. Mac burst into the foyer. Krock was a few steps behind him.

"You boys are just in time to catch the show," I said. "This is better than Laurel and Hardy."

"Mac! He's burning all the tapes!"

"What!" Mac shrieked and lurched in my direction. I leaped to my feet and brandished the poker at him. As I did, the marshmallow dislodged itself and sailed across the room, sticking fast against a framed Kandinsky poster from the Guggenheim museum.

"Take another step, Mac, and what I give you will make root canals feel like a French kiss."

He stopped dead. I bent down, grabbed more tapes, and fed them to the fire. There were perhaps a dozen cassettes remaining. Mac made a move but I checked him by raising the poker overhead and he froze in kind of a crouch. Bob remained behind him.

" . . . the attitude of many younger poets, like yourself, in terms of craft . . ." the image of a younger, more self-assured, less panicky Mac MacWhorter said over the TV screen.

"I'm not kidding," I told him. "I'll brain you one if you come any closer."

"He's gone insane, Mac! Don't move!" Cleo screamed.

I chucked more tapes in the fire. There was a *guuuuussssh* of yellow flame.

"Bob," Mac said quietly without moving his head. "Go into the kitchen and call the police."

"Don't bother, Krock," I said.

"Go *on*, Bob," Mac said through clenched teeth. Krock did go in there, via the other side of the foyer, but was back seconds later to report the damaged condition of the phone.

"The wires are all ripped to shit," he said.

"Okay, go upstairs. There's a phone in our bedroom," Mac said in a low, tension-filled voice.

"Drat!" I said. "Should have thought of that—"

"Have you thought of what kind of trouble you're in?"

"Not really."

"Then let me fill you in: you're going to jail, fella."

"You think so?"

"I'm absolutely certain."

I yelled through the foyer and up the stairs to Krock: "Tell them I want you arrested too. For wife-fucking. Tell them I've already got you under a citizen's arrest. And Mac also, for child molesting."

"Give me the poker, Schuster," Mac said in the same quiet voice he used with Krock. "Come on, let's have it." He extended his hand and began walking toward me. When he was a few steps away, I let him have it: right across the palm, as hard as I could. You could hear the bones crunch. Cleo screamed.

"Shut up!" I told her. Mac, in the meantime, had crumpled up on the floor, and was groaning and thrashing wildly on the carpet, his hand tucked between his legs. Krock came tearing down the stairs and around the corner.

"The cops are on their— holy shit! What'd you do to him?"

"He asked for it so I let him have it."

"So, you're going to add assault to the list of charges?"

"I dunno. I guess so."

On another whim, I grabbed the brandy bottle and pegged it at Krock's head with all my might. He dodged it adroitly, however, and it sailed into a framed watercolor on the wall. Both the glass-covered artwork and the bottle shattered into a million fragments.

"I've been toying with the idea of homicide, to tell you the truth."

"I feel sorry for you, hotshot. You just couldn't handle it, could you? You just had to blow it— and throw away your whole damn career too."

"What do you care about my career?"

"I thought you'd like to know, that's all."

"Well, you can sit on it. You call this a career! Pussy-Picking Time in Texas?"

Krock smirked uncomfortably.

"You fucking fraud," I said.

I bent down and chucked the last six remaining tapes into the fire. A cascade of smoldering black melted plastic goop was oozing over the hearth and dripping onto the polished wood floor beneath the raised lip of the fieldstone fireplace. The interview on the TV screen had concluded. The closing credits were rolling over the once-again silhouetted figures, and an inane sort of fifties-style be-bop jazz played in the background. I reared back and flung the heavy brass poker directly into the center of the screen. It exploded with a hollow-sounding *paa-thwock* and a grim little fanfare of sparks. Then I sat down in one of the chrome-and-leather easy chairs to await the police. Krock stood right where he was. Cleo flew past him and ran upstairs. Mac remained on the floor, groaning dismally and clutching his shattered hand. Outside, it was an effulgent winter morning and the sky was a brilliant azure above the naked trees.

nine

Boy, if *I* was ever in trouble and had to call the police I sure wouldn't want to depend on the Reddington force. It must have taken those yo-yos half an hour to get up to Mac's place. But when they finally did arrive, it was at full strength: three squad cars and eight officers, all armed with riot guns and helmets, not to mention the .357's strapped to their belts. One might have supposed that Sirhan Sirhan, Charles Whitman, Arthur Bremmer, Richard Franklin Speck, Charlie Manson and Juan Corona were having a bachelor party at Mac's place, the way those cops burst in.

I think they were disappointed to find me sitting quietly in a chair, eating marshmallows. I also think they *wanted* me to try some funny stuff, like an escape attempt, because a couple of them roughed me up and pushed me around while I docilely held out my hands for the cuffs. I didn't say much. I tried to be as polite and accommodating as possible.

They shoved me into the back seat of a squad car and drove me down to the station-house in a convoy, their sirens wailing absurdly all the way down the mountainside. Needless to say, they confiscated my marshmallows as "evidence."

I was fingerprinted and photographed and chucked into a cell of their admirable new slammer just as breakfast was being served to the other prisoners—three others, to be exact. Being a more high-toned criminal (and possibly even a more dangerous one) than their usual catch, I was shown to a cell of my very own, though I could hear a drunk lowing like a sick steer down the hall. It wasn't a bad jail at all. Modern, well-lighted, hygienic, it rather resembled a tidy new grammar school, with cheerful color schemes and the smell of fresh paint. It was a product of recent federal funding, I learned from a proud young officer. If the state penitentiary was half as nice, I thought, I wouldn't mind teaching *The Cat in the Hat* to Vermont's murderers, rapists, arsonists, bad check artists, and humpers of sheep. But these idle musings did not occupy me long. I ate a few plastic spoonfuls of the Rice Krispies they shoved under the bars of my cell, reeled backward to the comfortable bunk, and fell fast asleep.

I woke up at four o'clock in the afternoon. I had a headachy, dehydrated feeling from all the booze the night before and sucked about a gallon of water from the faucet of the built-in chromium washbasin. The hangover soon went away. In a little while, a guard clattered down the tiled hallway with a cartful of dinner trays and seeing me awake, sagely observed that I "was up," to which observation I agreed.

"I want to call my lawyer," I told him.

I was escorted down the hall to a kind of bare office. Soon a sergeant entered the little green room. He looked weary from a lifetime of writing traffic tickets and fighting communism, not to mention dealing with criminal lunatics like myself. There was a brief hassle about my making a long-distance call, but I explained how I would ask the operator for *time and charges* and told them they could confiscate the amount from my wallet, which had already been confiscated.

Since it was Saturday, I called Krezney at home, but the phone was answered by a tape recorder which instructed me to leave a message when it beeped.

"Uh, this is Richie Schuster, Paul. I'm calling from the Reddington town jail over here in Vermont. There are a bunch of charges. I'm not sure how many. Don't worry. Thank you. Beep."

For the next couple of hours, the other inmates and I got to know each other by chatting up and down the corridor from our cells. The acoustics were superb. The drunk was on his way to Burlington for psychiatric exams. He wasn't too hot on the idea. I told him not to worry, that psychiatry was the greatest thing since night baseball and that he could only benefit from it, anybody could, the sane as well as the emotionally troubled. He told me to blow it out my ass. I told him he was a fool to pass up free psychotherapy as long as the state was picking up the tab. Just talking to him, I said, I could tell he was a guy who wasn't living up to his potential. I related to him the story of how Harold Hughes, a former alcoholic, became governor of Iowa, and later, senator. He said he liked being a drunk and told me to go fuck myself.

The other two prisoners were a pair of teenage meatheads under arrest for robbing a hi-fi store. It was their third time in jail each, and they thought it was the height of hilarity. I did not feel as optimistic about them as I did about the drunk. They thought it was an even bigger riot when I said I was a professor at the college up on the mountain. They asked me if I got "a lot" up there. Heck, I told them, that was all we did up there. I said I was getting so much I didn't know whether to shit or go blind. For their amusement, I made up tales of orgies and fantastic sexual feats. Unfortunately, I was too successful, for after a while I realized by the sounds they were making that they were both jerking off. The drunk, in fact, advised me of their atrocious behavior. When I stopped with the tall tales, they called me an asshole and finished the dismal work on their own.

Around nine o'clock, the shifty-eyed, overweight sergeant shuffled back down and unlocked my cell. He said I had a visitor. I couldn't imagine who. We went down to the little, green room again. Annie Krock was waiting there.

The sergeant left us alone but kept his eye on me from outside via a window in the door, in case she slipped me a hand grenade or something. We sat there for a long time on opposite sides of the table, not saying anything. Annie's hair was braided and pinned on top of her head. Her eyes were red and baggy, as from extreme fatigue. I asked her for a smoke and she gave me one.

"It's all so awful," she said at last. "I'm afraid of what's going to happen to you."

"Don't worry, Annie. I'm not worried."

"It was in the *Valley News* today. Just a small item, but they put it on the front page. I'm sure President Bleeker knows."

"That's all right. I don't care," I said. "I'm sorry about the other night, Annie. What I did to you."

"I know you are."

"It wasn't really directed *at* you, if you can believe that."

"I know it wasn't."

I started blubbering again all of a sudden. It was strange, because up until that moment I was feeling curiously untroubled about *everything*. The feelings of release, of giddy gratification, following my night of lunacy were beginning to wear off and daunting reality was forcing its way back into my life. Annie stroked my head as I lay face down on the table, crying. Eventually, I pulled myself together and stopped.

"I wanted to tell you that I'm leaving Bob," she said. "I mean, I've left him."

"You have?"

"Yes."

"Because of Sally?"

"No."

"Oh."

"Because of . . . a lot of things."

"I'm sorry."

"So am I," she said with a sniffle. Her eyes were very moist. "I'm staying with Neda for the time being—"

"Uh-oh. . . ."

"Don't worry, Richie. She's a good friend. I just wanted to let you know. You can reach me there if you . . . if you need anything."

The sergeant came in and said that our time was up. Annie tried to smile pleasantly at him, but he did not return it, probably thinking that anybody who was a friend or relation of mine must ipso-facto be a creep or a Communist.

"It means a lot to me," I said. "You coming in here like this after—"

Annie swept around the table and squeezed me for a moment. My chin got wet where it brushed her cheek.

I told her I'd call her at Neda's when I got out. The sergeant showed her to the outer door.

You tell time in jail by your meals. Krezney materialized just before lunch on Sunday and was escorted to my cell by a young officer who told me I was free to go— on bail. In his usual, slovenly fashion, Krezney was dressed in a rumpled suit. It was a seersucker too, and inappropriate in the cold weather. But his sartorial defects were, after all, not only part of his charm as a human being, but a ruse to those suave tricksters among his profession who might stupidly underestimate his intelligence. I was glad to see the shifty old slob.

He was even heftier than the last time I saw him back in Cambridge, more than a year earlier. His walk was now a distinct waddle, but whereas with a smaller man it might have implied weakness, for Krezney it suggested the brute strength of a large bull walrus, and the long moustache he had grown on his broad Slavic face over the past year only enhanced this precise image. He walked, or rather waddled, with his head cocked slightly down and to the left, as it constantly in the act of charging. Even the policemen seemed to regard him as a purposeful and intimidating creature.

We drove in Krezney's Mercedes to the Depot, an old B & M railroad station that had been recently converted into a steakhouse. He ordered a gin and tonic. I noticed that he was perspiring. I was somewhat chilly, myself, and ordered an Irish coffee.

"They got some pretty serious charges against you, my friend," Paul began after our drinks arrived. He withdrew a small alligator-skin notebook from his jacket. "Want to hear them?"

"No."

"Let's see—"

"Don't tell me—"

"There's burglary, first degree, felony—that's for busting into this guy, whatsisname's—"

"MacWhorter."

"MacWhorter's house, and it includes assaulting him in the commission of a robbery. And we got unlawful imprisonment, first degree, another felony—that's for threatening this guy's wife. And we got criminal mischief, first degree, another felony, for burning this bird's tapes, on which he places a value in excess of $250,000—"

"He's full of shit."

"Possibly. And I think they're considering tacking on something like assault, second degree, which may sound a little redundant, but which is nevertheless another felony—for seeking to maim this guy—"

"You can stop now."

"I know. That's the end of the list. Unless they decide to get cute and throw in reckless endangerment just for the fun of it. Altogether, I'd say we're talking something like eight years, if you figure minimum con-current sentences and time off for good behavior, and, depending on the niceties of the Vermont penal codes, which I'm not entirely versed in and which may differ from what we got back in the Commonwealth. In short, you need one fucking rattlesnake of an attorney, which is how come I'm here."

"What was the bail?"

"I thought you preferred to remain ignorant."

"You've roused my curiosity."

"Ten thousand. Ten percent to the bondsman, of course. My hard-earned bread, that is. Ten grand might sound a little steep, but these woodchucks get greedy with you white-collar boys. If one of the yokels pulled this shit he'd be out for less than a grand."

"Thanks for bailing me out, Paul."

Krezney stared at me for a minute while the waitress set down our steaks. As soon as she turned her back on our table, he reached across and cuffed me lightly on the head.

"Such a schmuck!" he said. "I don't believe you."

"I'm weirder than you thought, huh?"

"Sheeeesh . . . !"

"Don't worry, Paul," I told him somewhat abstrusely and dug into my steak. I was famished after two days of Rice Krispies and Wonder Bread with margarine.

"I *am* worried, Richie. From what I can tell, these monkeys would like nothing better than to stick it to you."

"Let 'em try."

"You don't seem to understand. They're *doing* it."

"I've got the whole situation under control."

"You do, huh? That's what they always think when you spring 'em on bail. It's that illusory taste of freedom. Let me tell you something, pal, if you're thinking of skipping to South America, you can forget it. The extradition treaties are quite a bit stiffer than they used to be. And there would be the little matter of me being an accessory to your unlawful flight—"

"Paul. . . ." I scoffed at him.

He scowled back and stabbed his fork into his salad as if he was impaling some wimpy pain-in-the-ass prosecutor. Then, with a mouth full of greens and bright-orange salad dressing, he said, "The one thing you've got going for you is that you're obviously not the criminal type: no record, a steady job, academic degrees and credentials up the ass. Lucky for you this Republic is not the democracy it pretends to be. Of course the one thing you've got going *against* you is that apparently you committed all the acts they're charging you with. What do you have to say about that?"

"Nuts."

After the meal Krezney took me over to the police impoundment lot where the cops towed my car after Mac complained that, notwithstanding all my other crimes, I was blocking his driveway. Krezney told me to call him on Tuesday, by which time he expected to have more information on my necessary court appearances. I told him not to worry again and watched him drive away in the wine-colored Mercedes shaking his head in the rear window.

Sally was not in the house when I got there. I found her suitcases in a closet in the spare bedroom-cum-office and proceeded to pack them with the contents of her closet. It was a terrible procedure and remorse dogged me as I came across a familiar dress or the hiking boots that were the twins of my own. It was no time, however, for sentimental lapses.

When the suitcases were stuffed, I lugged them downstairs and set them in the middle of the living room rug. Then I sat down to wait. It was quite dark when I heard the Datsun pull into the driveway.

She put down the alpine rucksack which she used as a tote-bag on the table in the hallway, then took off her down jacket and hung it from a peg on the wall. She did not notice me sitting in the pool of darkness until she was halfway across the living room. She took the three remaining steps to the table with the lamp on it and switched it on before she spoke.

"Aren't you in enough trouble without coming over here and starting something else?" she said in that familiar sarcastic tone of voice which, once upon a time, I found irresistibly sexy, but which now sounded reckless, brazen.

"No," I replied.

"You blew it, Rich. Why not just face the facts, and stop bothering people."

I did not dignify the remark with a reply.

"Well," she continued, "you can't just sit there all night. I'm going into the kitchen to get myself a glass of wine. I will not be offering you a drink, and you are not invited to stick around. When I come back, I expect you to be gone."

She turned and started walking into the kitchen.

"Sally."

She stopped.

"Turn around, Sally."

She did, an impatient expression on her face and her arms crossed.

"Those bags on the floor are yours. They're all packed. Take them and get out of here."

"You've got a case," she sneered and started away again.

"Sally—"

"Oh what, for Chrissake!" she cried vehemently and stopped once again.

"I do have a case. You're going to leave this house. And I'll tell you why: because I'm in a position to create a whole heap of unpleasantness for that certain someone in your life."

"Don't make me laugh."

"Never could. Why start now?"

"When the courts are through with you, you're going to find out what the word *unpleasant* really means."

"There aren't going to be any courts."

"Oh no?" Sally said with a brief, false laugh and a defiant flip of her hair. She inserted a cigarette between her tightened lips.

"Oh, there'll be divorce court," I explained. "Don't worry about that. I'm not going to kill myself, or even you, in case that's what you're thinking. But this is what you need to do right now: take your suitcases, and go over to Bob's house, or wherever the hell he's staying, and ask him whatever happened to his Tarheel Hero."

"His what . . . ?"

I spelled it for her.

"What the hell is *that* supposed to mean?"

"He'll know."

"You mind explaining it to me?"

"Yes."

"Oh, you do, huh?"

"Yes. It's too complicated to go into. I'm sure you understand."

"What is it supposed to be? Some kind of threat?"

"That's right. Now, pick up your bags and get out."

"Why don't I just leave all this stuff here and go over and tell him what you said and then maybe we'll see about these bags."

"It would be better if you took them with you. Believe me, just this once."

She looked as if she was thinking it over for a minute. Then, she went to the hall, put on her goose-down jacket and returned to the living room. She tried the largest bag.

"It's heavy. Will you give me a hand?"

"No."

"How petty."

"I know. But it gives me a cheap thrill."

"Okay. Fuck you, Rich."

She dragged the first one out and returned momentarily for the two smaller ones. She left the door wide open on her way out again and it filled the room with cool, fresh air.

I was not at all surprised when the phone rang at 8:30 the following morning. But I was a little surprised to hear Mac's slightly nasal, Midwestern inflection instead of the more melodic Southern drawl I had expected.

"Schuster . . . ?"

"Yes."

"I'm not going to waste any time chatting, if you don't mind. Kindly draw up a letter of resignation and have it on my secretary's desk by noon. Is that clear?"

"I have a better suggestion—"

"Sorry. I don't care to hear it."

"Then maybe you better speak to the Tarheel Hero up the block. I'm sure he'll have the same suggestion."

There was a long silence at Mac's end of the line, though I could near him breathing. I was in no hurry.

Finally, in kind of a cracked whisper Mac said, "What's your suggestion?"

"Lunch."

"You're abominable."

"You ain't seen nothin' yet, fuckface. One o'clock at the Depot. Make sure Gomer Pyle joins us."

"Do you have any idea what you've done to the cause of contemporary American poetry?"

"I didn't know it was a cause."

"You disgust me."

"Wait until lunch, Mac. You'll really want to throw up then."

He hung up.

I arrived deliberately fifteen minutes late. The restaurant had a busy luncheon crowd. Since the owners made it a point to shut out all natural daylight, it was quite dim inside and it took a moment for my eyes to adjust. Then I saw them: they were sitting hunched together at a corner table beneath an enormous engraving in an ornate gilded frame. The engraving depicted a sort of Natty Bumppo woodsman character standing over a slain catamount, bloodied knife in hand. They did not see me at the bar and I watched them for a moment.

Bob said something to Mac and I saw him slap the table for emphasis, though I could not hear it for the murmur of conversation and the clatter of plates and silverware. Mac shook his head in apparent reply. Bob retorted sharply, possibly an expletive or two, and looked in my direction. I edged past a waitress toward their table. Krock had a bottle of Miller's in front of him and Mac was drinking Scotch. Mac was also wearing a brand-new plaster cast on his right arm. Snow white and as yet unautographed, it extended from his elbow to the second knuckles of his hand. Under each fingertip could be seen a curved aluminum splint.

"You guys order yet, or what?" I inquired, rubbing my hands expectantly and taking a seat. Bob sort of shrank away from me, as if I smelled bad, and muttered something that sounded like *Jesus*.

"If you think we're going to linger over lunch with you, you're crazy," Mac said.

"Hey, we already know that. What further proof do you need. By the way, would you like me to autograph your cast—?"

Mac stood up, but Bob grabbed the hem of his corduroy sport jacket and yanked him back down to his seat.

"I didn't come here for a charade," Mac told Bob angrily.

"Yeah, well I figured he'd jerk us off first," Bob said.

"Oh, I'm not jerking you off. I'm going to give it to you right up the ass, so relax and think about what you'd like to order for lunch."

The waitress brought us our menus—three huge slabs of slate with the bill of fare written carefully in chalk.

"The stuffed shrimp's good," she said earnestly, "and the fish of the day is broiled scrod."

I ordered a "Cowcatcher Special," a sixteen-ounce steak. Mac ordered a bowl of soup and Bob asked for a cheeseburger. I tried to engage them in some chit-chat while waiting for the food to arrive, but it was no go. Nor were they particularly voluble during the meal itself. Mac was too busy gnashing his teeth to eat his soup and Bob did not care to comment on my observations about the National Football League. When they tried to get down to cases, I made it a point to change the subject. Eventually, the waitress returned to see how we were doing.

"Gosh, I'd like some dessert."

"Oh, for Christ's—"

"What's good?" I asked the waitress.

"Cheesecake, apple pie with or without ice cream, chocolate mousse. It's made on the premises."

"Which is?"

"The mousse."

"Really? I'll have the pie, then. And some brandy."

"Coffee?"

"You bet."

"All the way around?"

"No thank you," Mac snarled. Bob shook his head.

After I finished the pie, and while I savored the Cognac and the coffee, I took three folded eight-by-eleven sheets of paper out of my jacket pocket and handed them to Bob, who examined them with disgust and passed them, in turn, to Mac. They were xerox copies of the first three pages of *Tarheel Hero*.

"Look familiar?" I asked.

"Where's the original?"

"In a stamped, sealed envelope addressed to President Bleeker with a letter explaining the contents in as dispassionate a manner as possible. Anonymous, of course, but with instructions as to how verification might be obtained."

Mac squirmed uncomfortably in his seat. A drop of sweat made a damp track between his cheekbone and his carefully groomed beard. Krock pursed his lips and tapped the table with his fingertips.

"You haven't mailed it yet?" Mac asked.

"Not yet," I said.

"What's your proposal, then?"

"I was kind of wondering what yours might be."

"This is blackmail, you know."

"I know."

"What if I tell you to go ahead and mail it?"

"Then I'll mail it."

Mac pushed himself slightly away from the edge of the table and leaned back in his chair. But the smirk he was working so energetically to sustain was betrayed by involuntary twitches and spasms of the other facial muscles. Krock, meanwhile, shifted his weight back and forth, rubbing his chin first with one hand, then with the other, his dark eyes flashing furtively.

"Look, Mac," he finally said, "I'm not figuring to screw around on this. Just tell him what he wants to hear—"

"Let him mail it—"

"Tell him!" Bob growled.

"How could you be so goddamned stupid to keep that thing around?" Mac shot back.

"Pride of ownership," Bob muttered hatefully. "Now, you tell him what he wants to hear or you'll be wearin' a cast on your other arm."

Mac's eyes seemed to glaze over. His face twitched more violently than before. All the color seemed to drain from his head. He looked like a man undergoing rapid and momentous hormonal changes.

"I'm prepared to drop all the charges," he said in a voice barely loud enough to hear.

"I thought you'd see it my way in the long run," I told him. "Now, when you've accomplished that with the local law enforcement people, I want you to go to Boston—"

"What?"

"—and go to this man's office, both of you." I handed Mac a slip of paper with Paul Krezney's name and business address on it. "This man is my attorney. Mac, I want you to be prepared to give a deposition stating that you mistakenly burned your own tape recordings while intoxicated and consequently fell and injured your hand while so doing. Okay?"

"What's the point?"

"Civil self-protection."

"How cunning."

"One must take care."

"What do I have to go for?" Bob asked.

"I was about to get to that. I want you to be prepared to give a deposition too: a guilt-ridden confession to the effect that you have been dicking my wife behind my back for six months and are compelled by conscience to come forward on behalf of the truth. You see, my wife has some nutty idea that I deserve to be crucified to pay for her sins. Don't ask me to explain it. I think it's some Aryan purification ritual or something. Anyway, it'll make things a whole lot easier for me when you get that done."

"It wasn't six months."

"However many it was will do fine."

"More like a year."

"Well, I hope you enjoyed yourself."

"I did."

"And I hope you enjoy yourself in court when Annie reams you. In fact, I know an excellent divorce attorney I think I'll put her on to."

"And you can kiss my ass."

"I think I'll pass, thank you."

We could have gone on in that vein forever, but I was personally finding it tedious. Instead, I informed them both that when Krezney notified me that the charges were dropped and the depositions completed, I would deliver the manuscript back to Bob's office at the English department. Then I left the two of them at the table with the check, and with each other for company.

That is nearly all there is to tell. Ten days later, our formal separation went into effect. Sally and Krock moved into a garden apartment down in the valley. She returned to the old farmhouse a few times to remove various personal items that I had been unable to cram into her suitcases. It was painful just being around her and we did not speak a word to each other on any of these occasions. It may startle you to hear that a part of me was still hopelessly in love with her. Anyway, after that, I saw virtually nothing of her. It snowed for month after month.

In April, when the landscape began to shift and heave with intimations of new life, I learned that Sally had split from Krock and had moved to Washington. I learned this not from either of the principals, nor anyone else in Reddington, but from the ever-vigilant Krezney, whose business it still was to keep track of her whereabouts pending our divorce.

Though I was naturally curious, and though our paths crossed now and again on campus, I did not ask Bob Krock what had transpired between the two of them and what brought the liaison to so untimely an end. For all his own character defects, I supposed that Krock had met his match in Sally, as Mac MacWhorter had on that luminous, but hair-raising, July evening now so long ago, and as I suppose I once did at an even more faraway Georgetown party.

Mac, like the imperishable cockroach which adapts to any change in its habitat, survived the loss of his precious tape collection and also the subsequent confusion and embarrassment over the exact cause of the calamity, as he will no doubt survive everything except the final scythe sweep of his personal harvestman. At last report, he was frantically booking interviews with America's leading poets before they all died of alcoholism.

I was not fired from my post as assistant professor of English. It would be nice to think that I played out my option, like a shrewd ballplayer, but the simple truth is that no contract was forthcoming for the next academic year. I learned eventually that this was President Bleeker's work. It seems that Dr. Bleeker was not fooled by any of the arrangements made between Mac and me following my night of terror. Oddly enough, though, informed sources let me know that while Lyman Bleeker did not at all approve of my destruction, he did seem to derive some perverse pleasure from the escapade in general, and enjoyed relating the story of my "goofy antics" to visiting friends.

Elsewhere across the campus, the strangest rumors and wild stories cropped up, especially among the students. One of them cast Mac, Krock and me in a homosexual triangle and suggested that I wrecked Mac's house as a "jilted lover." Another story pegged me as an insatiable satyr and cad who *drove* his long-suffering wife into the arms of that gallant Carolinian, Robertson Krock! The weirdest one hypothesized a campus-wide wife-swapping society along the lines of Tichnor and Shank's old model, and struck me as wonderfully quaint.

Anyway, I was sacked by default. But I was sacked.

I did call Annie Krock at Neda Nagy's house, and though I had serious misgivings about the symmetry of it, I began to spend a great deal of time with her, and after New Years, Annie moved into the old farmhouse with me for my last semester at Reddington.

She is still with me, here in the old gristmill outside Manchester, Vermont, which we bought the following Autumn and which we have been restoring, believe it or not, with federal funds. Annie has been a terrific help making all those applications to national and international organizations just dying to give away grant money. For instance, the *Institut für Amerikanische Geschichte* paid me $5,000 for a study of German-American fiction. The John Simon Guggenheim Memorial Foundation coughed up seven grand for an epic poem about Ethan Allen and the Green Mountain Boys. The National Endowment for the Arts kept me in groceries for a year when I agreed to furnish them with a Bicentennial play about the Battle of Reddington. It was performed on a showboat that traveled up and down the Hudson River during the summer of '76. There has been a veritable windfall of lesser gifts and handouts from other sources, so all tolled, my income has been about equal to what it would have been if I stuck to teaching.

Honniker—you remember him, don't you?—went from a wheat farm, to a used car lot, to a tropical fish store, to a Tudor-style suburban home on a quiet lane in Oyster Bay, Long Island. Yes, in a strange way, Honniker became myself, and while the novel is by no means strict autobiography, I am at least writing about things I know—as Sally, it turns out, correctly admonished me on that grim night long ago. I did get him past the first chapter this time too. The first draft is almost complete, but I'm in no hurry to finish.

Annie is a good woman. No one could be less like Sally Parsifal. Where Sally was tough, Annie is tender. Where Sally was a wise guy, Annie is thoughtful. Where Sally was an adversary, Annie is a partner. Where I loved Sally with a love that knew no logic, I love Annie logically. Never again do I want to lose my head. Aren't all compromises fundamentally sad?

It was Chesmire who helped me keep things pasted together in the grim, anticlimactic months that followed my grand outburst. Poor Chesmire, who murdered himself—committed suicide—at least according to his own theory of the human will. The newspapers put it a little differently. They said he was cut down in his driveway by a shotgun blast from a passing automobile. The next day, the state police apprehended as their prime suspect: a forty-one-year-old white male named Don DeCamp, the manager of a Rutland footwear manufacturing concern. That's right: Don the wife beater, Gloria's husband, who was never too fond of psychiatrists to begin with, but who took particular umbrage over an extracurricular form of therapy which Chesmire was practicing in various motels with the wife in question. So, he blew poor Chesmire away.

I shall miss him a lot. Chesmire must have wanted it

to happen, though. Had he survived the attack, I'm sure he would agree. To him, man's nature was his will, and his will alone. And the will, to Chesmire, was each man's alone, so that life was essentially a wish.

As pure theory, I suppose this has its charms, but life is not theory and I'm not at all sure that I believe it is a wish either.

In the end, I'll go along with those anonymous savants of the Encyclopedia Britannica who call human nature "indescribable," shrug their shoulders in unison, and quit while they are ahead. If it's enlightenment you're after, stick to the back roads. And watch out for the baboons.